Forever Too Far

Also by

ABBI GLINES

THE SEABREEZE SERIES

Breathe

Because of Low

While it Lasts

Just for Now

Fallen Too Far

Never Too Far

The Vincent Boys

The Vincent Brothers

Forever Too Far

Abbi Glines

SIMON AND SCHUSTER

First published in Great Britain in 2013 by Simon & Schuster UK Ltd
A CBS COMPANY

3 5 7 9 10 8 6 4

Simon & Schuster UK Ltd
1st Floor
222 Gray's Inn Road
London
WC1X 8HB

Simon & Schuster Australia, Sydney

Simon & Schuster India, New Delhi

A CIP catalogue copy for this book is available
from the British Library.

ISBN: 978-1-4711-2002-2
Ebook ISBN: 978-1-4711-2003-9

Printed and bound by CPI Group (UK) Ltd, Croydon, CR0 4YY

www.simonandschuster.co.uk
www.simonandschuster.com.au

Abbi loves to hear from her readers. You can connect with her on
Facebook: Abbi Glines (Official Author Page)
Twitter: @abbiglines
Website: www.abbiglines.com

"When you find your reason for living, hold onto it. Never let it go. Even if it means burning other bridges along the way."

– Rush Finlay

PROLOGUE

If I hadn't been so taken in by Blaire and the way she lit up the place, I would have seen him walk in. But I hadn't. It wasn't until the talking surrounding me went silent and eyes all stared at the door my back was to. Glancing down at Blaire who was still talking to Woods and didn't notice the change in the room, I moved her behind me in a protective measure before turning around to see what had captured the bars attention.

The same silver eyes that I saw every day in the mirror were focused on me. It had been awhile since I'd seen my dad. Normally we kept in contact more but with Blaire coming into my world and completely turning it on its axis, I hadn't taken the time and energy to track my father down so I could talk to him.

It looked like he had come to find me this time.

"That's your father," Blaire said quietly beside me. She'd

moved from where I'd tucked her behind me and was holding onto my arm now.

"Yeah, it is."

BLAIRE

Without stage makeup and black leather clothing he looked like an older version of Rush. I had to move quickly to keep up with Rush who had my hand clasped tightly in his as he walked swiftly outside away from the other guests in the bar. His father led the way. I wasn't sure if Rush was happy to see him or not. The only interaction they'd had was Rush nodding his head towards the door. He obviously hadn't wanted this introduction to have an audience.

Dean Finlay, the world's most notorious drummer, stopped several times on our way out to autograph items being shoved in front of him. It wasn't just females either. One guy had even stepped forward and asked him to sign a bar napkin. The threatening gleam in Rush's eyes as he tried to get his father out of the bar kept the rest of them away. Instead, they all remained silent and watched as Slacker Demon's drummer headed out the door.

The night breeze was cold now. I immediately shivered and Rush stopped and wrapped his arms around me. "We need to go to the house. I'm not going to make her stand out here and talk. It's too damn cold." Rush told his father.

Dean finally stopped walking and looked back at me. His eyes slowly took me in and I could see the moment he noticed my stomach.

"Dean, this is Blaire Wynn. My fiancée. Blaire, this is Dean Finlay, my father." Rush said in a tight voice. He didn't sound like he wanted to make this introduction.

"No one told me I was gonna be a grandpa," Dean said in a slow drawl. I wasn't sure how he felt about that because there was no emotion on his face.

"I've been busy," was the only response Rush gave him. That was odd. Was he embarrassed to tell his dad? I felt sick in my stomach and started to ease away from him.

His arms tightened their hold on me and I could feel his attention focused completely on me. "What's wrong?" Rush asked, turning his back on his father and bending down so he could look me directly in the eyes.

I didn't want to have this conversation in front of Dean. I could feel his dad's eyes on both of us. I shook my head but my body was still tense. I couldn't help that. The fact he hadn't told his father was bothering me.

"I'm taking her to the car. I'll meet you back at the house," Rush said over his shoulder but kept his eyes focused on mine. I dropped my gaze wishing I hadn't reacted now. I was

making a scene. Dean was going to think I was a whinny princess.

I opened my mouth to argue when Rush wrapped his arm around my waist and led me to the Range Rover. He was anxious. He didn't like me upset, which was something we needed to work on. I would get upset. He couldn't control that.

Rush opened the passenger side door and lifted me up and put me in like I was five. When he thought I was upset he started treating me like a child. We really needed to work on that too.

He didn't even have his door closed before he looked at me. "Something is wrong. I need to know so I can fix it."

I sighed and sank back against the seat. I might as well get this over with even if I was being a little touchy. "Why haven't you told your dad about the baby?"

Rush reached over and closed his hand over mine. "That's what's wrong? You're upset because I haven't told Dean?"

I nodded and kept my eyes on our hands resting on my leg.

"I haven't taken time to track him down. And I knew he'd show up when I told him because he'd want to meet you. I wasn't ready for company just yet. Especially him."

I was being silly. Lately my emotions were on high alert. I lifted my eyes and met his concerned gaze. "Okay. I understand that."

Rush leaned over and kissed my lips gently. "I'm sorry I upset you," he whispered before pressing one more kiss to the corner of my lips and leaning back. It was moments like these that I became a swoony mess.

"He's here now. So, let's go see what brought him here before my mother finds out. I want you to myself. I don't like having my fucked up family around."

Rush didn't let go of my hand as he cranked the engine and pulled out onto the road. I laid my head against the seat and turned it so I could look at him. His unshaven jaw made him look older and untamed. Very sexy. I wish he'd not shave more often. I liked the way it felt too. He had taken out his earring and hardly ever wore it anymore.

"Why do you think he's here?" I asked

Rush glanced over at me. "I was hoping he was here to meet you. But I don't think he knew about you yet. He looked surprised. So that means this could very well be about Nan."

Nan. His sister hadn't been back to Rosemary since she was released from the hospital. Rush didn't seem to be worried about it but he loved his sister. I hated being the reason she stayed away. Now that she knew who her real father was and that I had never taken anything away from her, I'd hoped we could be friends for Rush's sake. It wasn't looking like that was going to happen.

"Do you think Nan has gone to see Kiro?" I asked.

Rush shrugged. "I don't know. She seems different since her accident."

The car came to a stop outside the large beach house that had been purchased for Rush by his father when he was just a kid. Rush squeezed my hand. "I love you, Blaire. I'm so damn proud

of the fact you're going to be the mother of my son. I want everyone to know. Never doubt that."

My eyes stung with tears and I nodded before picking up his hand kissing it. "I get emotional. You need to ignore me when I get like that."

Rush shook his head. "I can't ignore you. I want to reassure you."

The passenger side door opened and I jerked my head around to see Dean Finlay standing there with a smirk on his face. "Let the woman out of the car, son. It's time I met the mother of my grandchild."

Dean held out his hand and I put mine in his not sure what else to do. His long fingers wrapped around my hand and he helped me down out of the Range Rover. Rush was there immediately, taking my hand from his father's and pulling me over to him. His dad chuckled and shook his head. "I'll be damned."

"Let's get inside." Rush replied.

RUSH

Dean walked over to the sofa and sank down on it before pulling out a pack of cigarettes. *Shit*. He was not what I wanted to deal with right now. "Can't smoke in here, or around Blaire for that matter. It's bad for the baby."

Dean cocked one of his eyebrows. "Hell boy, I'm pretty damn sure your momma smoked cigarettes when she was pregnant with you."

I had no doubt that she did that and more. Didn't mean my kid was going to be exposed to that stuff. "Doesn't mean it's healthy. Blaire is nothing like Mom."

At the mention of her name, Blaire walked into the living room carrying two beers. I hadn't asked her to get them. I didn't like to see her wait on anyone. But she did it anyway. I walked over and met her halfway. "You didn't have to get these," I told her taking them from her hands as I placed a kiss on her temple.

"I know. But we have a guest. I want him to feel welcome."

The sweet smile on her lips made it hard to concentrate on my dad. I wanted to take her up to the bedroom.

"Bring me the beer boy and stop being so damn overbearing. You're gonna smother the girl. Don't know what the fuck has gotten into you."

A small bubble of laughter came from Blaire's lips and I decided since he'd made her laugh, I'd overlook his words.

"Here," I said, shoving the beer his way. "Now, why're you here?"

"What? Can't a dad come see his son when he wants to?"

"It's Rosemary. You never come here."

Dean shrugged and took a swig of his beer then threw an arm over the back of the sofa and propped both his feet up on the coffee table and crossed them at the ankle. "Your sister is a crazy bitch. She's *fucking insane*. We need help."

It was about Nan. I'd thought it might be. I sat down on the chair across from him and held my hand out to Blaire. I didn't want her standing and I wanted her to feel welcome in our conversation. She walked over to me and I pulled her down on to my lap. "What has Nan done?" I asked, almost afraid to hear the answer.

Dean took another long swig of his beer. Then ran his hand through his long shaggy hair. "Question is, what hasn't she done. Damn girl is raising hell. We can't get any rest. We finished up the tour two weeks ago and came back to LA to enjoy some down time. She showed up and all hell broke loose.

No one is getting any down time. Kiro doesn't know what to do with her. We need some help."

I knew Nan had been quiet, but I hadn't expected her to go to LA and search Kiro out. She knew my dad and Kiro shared a Beverly Hills mansion. They'd been living in it when they weren't touring all my life. Kiro had been married a couple times and he'd moved out during those times, but after each divorce he came back. It was known as the Slacker Demon mansion. No one was every really sure which band members were in residence at the time.

"Is she staying at the mansion?" I asked.

Dad raised his eyebrows. "Do I look like an idiot to you? Fuck no, she isn't staying there. She just shows up all the damn time. She's making demands and shit. Kiro has tried to ease things over and form some sort of relationship with her, but she won't let him. She won't listen and she . . . well, she found out he has another daughter. Didn't go over well."

Apparently she didn't know about Kiro's son yet either but then Mase never came around.

"She must be so upset," Blaire said with actual concern in her voice. How Blaire could feel any sympathy for Nan I didn't know. "You need to go see her. Help her deal with this and see if you can't help her and Kiro form some sort of relationship." I started to disagree but Dean cut me off.

"I like her already. That's exactly what you need to do. Your room is empty and you know it's comfortable. Bring Blaire with you and that'll give me a chance to get to know her and spend time with you as well. If you don't, Kiro may end up killing Nan."

Blaire squeezed my shoulder. "I think we should go. Nan needs you."

I tilted my head back and looked up at her. "Why do you care what Nan needs?" I asked in awe.

"Because you love her," was her simple reply.

"This one's a keeper. Now, enough about Nan. I wanna know when this baby is due and when the wedding is." Dean said with a cheerful tone. Very different from the one he was using when he spoke about Nan.

Blaire looked over at my dad and smiled. "I'm twenty weeks pregnant. The baby isn't due until mid April. As for the wedding, we were going to get married in two weeks but I don't want this to be weighing on Rush. I'd rather put the wedding off and let him deal with family issues first. We haven't mailed out invitations or anything. So changing the date isn't a problem."

"No. I'm not waiting any longer to change your last name," I argued, but Blaire put her finger over my lips.

"Shhh. I don't want to argue about this. I can't enjoy our wedding knowing you have family issues to deal with. Let's enjoy Thanksgiving with our friends like we'd planned and then go to LA and deal with Nan. Once you have all that behind you, then we can focus on our wedding."

I didn't want to wait. I hated the idea of her still being Blaire Wynn while our baby grew inside her. I wanted her to have my name and the world to know I wanted her and my baby. But the determined gleam in her eyes told me I wasn't going to win this argument.

"I just want you to be happy," I finally replied.

Blaire kissed the tip of my nose. "I know you do. One of the many reasons I love you."

"If you're waiting until after Thanksgiving to head back to LA and deal with that sister of yours, then so am I. Besides, it's been years since I spent a Thanksgiving with you," my dad announced.

I wasn't sure how I felt about that.

"We would love to have you here, Mr. Finlay," Blaire informed him smiling brightly like she really meant it. Fuck. I was gonna have to let this happen.

"Just call me Dean, sweetheart. We're already family."

The pleased look in her eyes made me smile. Maybe having my dad around for Thanksgiving wouldn't be so bad after all. If he could make Blaire smile then I'd deal with it.

BLAIRE

Talking about Thanksgiving had reminded me of my mother. This would be my first holiday without her. The more that sank in, the harder it became to breathe. I forced a smile and made my excuses before rushing upstairs to take a shower. Rush needed some alone time with his dad anyway.

I let the tears I'd held back fall freely as I undressed and stepped into the shower. The warm water rained down over me as a sob broke free. Last year I had cooked our Thanksgiving meal and we had eaten it together in the dining room. No friends or family. Just the two of us. I'd cried that night too. Because deep down I'd known this was my last Thanksgiving with my mother. The memories of years gone by when Valerie and Dad had been there were bittersweet. My heart ached for all we'd lost. I hadn't thought anything could hurt as badly but I knew now that I was wrong.

Facing the holiday without my mom was going to be hard. She loved Thanksgiving and Christmas. We would always start decorating the house for Christmas on Thanksgiving Day. Then we'd sit down and watch *White Christmas* together that evening while we ate left over turkey and sweet potato casserole. It had been our tradition. Even after we lost Valerie and Dad had left us.

This year everything would be different. Knowing Rush would be with me and that I was starting a new family of my own eased the ache. I just wished my mother were here to see me this happy.

The door opened and I spun around to see Rush walk into the bathroom. He was frowning. He stopped when he saw me and studied me a moment before pulling his shirt off and throwing it onto the marble floor. Then he unsnapped his jeans and stepped out of them and his boxer briefs. I watched as he stepped into the shower.

"Why're you crying?" he asked, cupping my face in his hands. I knew the shower had washed away my tears but my eyes must still be red.

I shook my head and smiled at him. I didn't want to worry him with my emotions.

"I heard you when I opened the door to the bedroom. I need to know why, Blaire."

I sighed and laid my head against his chest then wrapped my arms around his waist. I had lost a lot but God had made up for that by giving me Rush. I needed to remember just how blessed

I really was. "The fact that this is my first Thanksgiving without my mom kind of hit me." I admitted.

Rush's arms tightened around me. "I'm sorry, baby," he whispered into my hair as he held me.

"Me too. She would've loved you. I wish you could have met her."

"I wish I could have too. I'm sure she was as perfect as you are."

Smiling I wanted to disagree. I was nowhere near as perfect as my mother. She was one of those special people that the world doesn't see often.

"If my dad being here is going to be hard on you, I'll send him away. I want to make this a good memory for you. Anything I can do to help you just tell me and I'll do it."

Tears trickled freely down my face again. Stupid pregnancy hormones made me a leaking fountain lately. "Having you with me makes it all better. Just talking about it made it sink in. Momma loved Thanksgiving. I knew last year it was the last one we'd spend together. The entire day I'd done everything I could to make it special for her. And me. I knew I'd need that memory."

Rush rubbed small circles on my back and held me in silence. We stood there while the water ran over us for several minutes. Finally he pulled back enough to look down at me. "Can I bathe you?" he asked.

I nodded unsure what he meant. He reached for one of the clean washcloths stacked up outside the shower and picked up one of my bottles of body wash. Then he began washing my back and shoulders. He picked up each of my arms as if I were a child and washed them thoroughly. I stood there and watched him as he concentrated on cleaning every inch of my body. He didn't make it sexual which surprised me. Instead, it was more sweet and innocent than anything else we'd ever done. His hand didn't linger as he washed between my legs. He only pressed his lips to my stomach once as he knelt in front of me and washed my legs and feet.

Once he was finished he stood up and began rinsing my body with his hands. Each touch seemed almost reverent. As if he were worshiping me instead of washing me. When my body was clean he then moved to my hair. I closed my eyes as his hands massaged my scalp. My knees went a little weak from the pleasure of it. Rush quickly rinsed the shampoo from my hair and then did my conditioning giving it just as much attention before running my hair under the clean water again.

My body was relaxed from the pampering. I was almost sluggish. Rush turned off the water and reached for two large towels. One he wrapped in my hair and the other one he wrapped around my body. Then he picked me up and carried me to the bed and laid me down.

"Just rest. I'll be right back," he whispered before kissing my forehead and walking back to the bathroom. The view of his naked ass was tempting and I wanted to stay awake. Having him touch me that way had turned me on even if that hadn't been his intention. I tried to wait on him but my eyes grew heavy and I faded away.

I snuggled deeper into the warmth. It smelled of sunshine and ocean air. Sighing contentedly I rubbed my cheek against the comforting warmth. It chuckled.

My eyes opened and Rush's bare chest was pressed up against my face. Smiling I kissed it and peered up at him. The amused smirk on his lips only made me giggle.

"You're like a little kitten in the mornings," he said with a deep husky voice. He must have just woken up too.

"If you didn't feel so good I wouldn't be searching you out to rub up against you in my sleep."

Rush winked. "Then I'm glad I feel good because your sweet ass isn't going to be rubbing against anyone else. I'd have to kill someone."

I loved this man.

"I'm sorry I fell asleep so quickly last night."

Rush shook his head. "Don't be. I love knowing I relaxed you and it was easy for you to fall asleep. I don't like seeing you sad."

I loved this man a whole damn lot.

Stretching against him I slipped both hands behind his neck and pressed my body against his. I squeezed my legs from the tingle of anticipation when his erection brushed my upper thigh. I needed him this morning. After the sweet moment last night I needed to feel completely connected now.

"Make love to me," I whispered, tucking my head in the crook between his neck and shoulder.

"My pleasure," he murmured and slipped his hand in between my thighs. He lifted one of my legs up and rested it on his hip. I was wide open and the exposed feeling excited me. His fingers grazed the inside of my thighs only teasing me by barely brushing just at my swollen needy entrance. I whimpered hoping to hurry him up but he would not be deterred. Instead it seemed to make him worse. His rough fingertips traced patterns from my knees up to the very top of my thigh then back again.

I was positive that his play had caused me to get embarrassingly wet. "Rush, please."

"Please what, sweet Blaire. What do you want me to do?"

I'd told him what I wanted already. Apparently, he wanted to hear more. Rush and his naughty talk always excited me. "Touch me."

"I am touching you," he replied.

"Touch me higher," I begged. He wanted me to talk dirty. I was going to tease him too.

He ran his finger in the crease of my thigh and I gripped his arms tightly and trembled. He was so close. "Here?" he asked.

I shifted so that his finger slipped closer. He started to move his hand away and stopped. "Fuck," he moaned, sliding his finger into me slowly. "So wet. I can't tease you when you're already so wet," he whispered.

I cried out as he gently ran his fingertip over my clit. He had me spread open and now having his hands touching me only made me crazier. I wanted more.

"My sweet girl was so ready for me," he said, moving two fingers inside of me and pressing against my g-spot.

The loud cry of pleasure that ripped out of me was more than he could handle. He grabbed my waist and positioned me over him before slowly sinking me down over his cock. "Damn, how'd it get tighter?" he growled, squeezing my hips and rocking against me as I sat down on him taking every inch inside me. This was what I'd wanted. To be full. Of Rush.

RUSH

Blaire wouldn't agree to my idea of staying up in my room naked all day. She insisted we get dressed and visit with Dean. I was of the opinion he'd understand my desire to stay locked away with Blaire but she disagreed. Just proved what little she knew of my father's rock star life.

I left her drying her hair and headed downstairs to start fixing breakfast. She hadn't eaten much last night at the party then she'd come home and gone to sleep before she could eat.

Dean was standing in my kitchen pulling out items from the fridge and sitting them on the island. I stood there and watched him a moment trying to figure out what he was doing. He sat the milk out then paused and looked over at me.

"Good morning. I wasn't sure you'd be coming out of the bedroom today the way you'd chased her upstairs last night when she left. I was going to tempt you both with breakfast."

I leaned back against the counter and crossed my arms over my chest. "I tried to keep her upstairs with me. She insisted we come visit with you," I explained.

Dean chuckled. "Like father, like son."

"I'm nothing like you. The woman I got pregnant happens to be my heart. I'll marry her and spend the rest of my life doing everything I can to make her smile."

Dean closed the fridge door and studied me. I could tell he hadn't expected words like those to come out of my mouth. The last time I'd spent time with him I'd had a different girl in my bed every night.

"What makes her different? You've been with a lot of girls. Why her?" If he wasn't honestly curious, I'd have been pissed. But he only knew me before Blaire.

"When she walked into my house the first time and I laid eyes on her I was attracted to her. That part was easy. But then I got to know her. She wasn't like any other girl I'd ever known. She was so determined when she should have been beat down. Her life had given her shit and she was fighting to live. She wasn't going to back down or give up. I admired her. Then I got a taste and I was sunk. She's everything I want to be."

A slow smile spread across Dean's face and then he nodded. "Well alright then. Guess you know more about life than your old man 'cause ain't no woman ever made me feel like that. I'm glad you found it. That's rare boy, so hang on tight. It won't come around again."

I never intended to let go. Dean looked around the room. "Where's the mixing bowls. I'm gonna make the momma of my grandkid some scrambled eggs."

My heart squeezed. "Second shelf to the left of the stove."

"You get the bacon going. She needs protein," he said as he got down a bowl.

I wasn't going to argue. I always made sure she ate properly in the mornings. "She will want a waffle too. I have a waffle iron for those," I told him.

Dean nodded. "Good to know you've been taking care of her."

We worked in silence for a few minutes. I wanted to ask about Nan and Kiro but I didn't want Blaire to walk down here and that be the first thing she heard. I liked her to enjoy her breakfast. Speaking about Nan was never a pleasant experience.

"Guess you know that Grant's been seeing Nan," Dean said as he whisked the eggs.

I froze. *What?* Had I just heard him correctly?

"I warned him she was as crazy as her momma and he needed to run like hell. I know she's your sister and you love her, but the girl is poison. Boy like Grant don't need that. He's always been a good kid. Hate to see her chew him up and spit him out."

I still couldn't find words. Grant and Nan. . . . how the fuck had that happened? If anyone knew how unstable Nan was then it was Grant. He'd grown up watching the shit she'd been handed from my mom and the father that never acknowledged her.

"Grant tried to come talk to her but she ran off with some guy she'd met at a club right in front of him. I think he's done. Washed his hands of that. I hope so."

I finally set down the waffle mix I'd been standing there holding as I stared at my dad like he was speaking gibberish. "Grant . . . was with Nan?" the disbelief in my voice got Dean's attention. He turned to look back at me.

"Yeah. Guessing from the look on your face you didn't know. Been dating for awhile from what I can tell. Poor guy looked really into her. But she's just like her momma. He's lucky to get out now."

"How?"

Dean shook his head. "I wondered the same thing."

I couldn't talk about this with him. I walked out of the kitchen and towards the double doors leading out onto the back porch. Once I was outside I pulled out my phone and dialed Grant's number. We told each other everything. Yet he'd been dating my sister and never said a word.

"Hey, bro." His chipper voice greeted me.

"I know about Nan," was all I said.

Grant let out a weary sigh. "I was hoping I'd be able to tell you about it. I wanted to. I just . . . she didn't want me to, then she had the accident. Then well . . . it's over. She's made it very clear that she doesn't want anything serious with me. I can't deal with her sleeping around. It wasn't just a booty call. I'd have never done that with Nan. You know that. I really liked her. Maybe I cared too much."

I sank down onto the chair beside me and stared out at the ocean. "Why didn't you tell me?"

"I wanted to. She begged me not to. I cared about her, Rush. I wanted it to work. I did what she asked. But I felt like shit lying to you about it."

He had cared about Nan? Wow.

"Dean says you're done with her now."

"She's done with me. I can't play her games."

I loved my sister but I also loved Grant. She'd break his heart. She wasn't good for him. My dad was right. Grant needed someone that could love him. I wasn't sure Nan could. Relief that he was ending it with her wasn't because I didn't want them together, but because I hated to think of Nan doing to Grant what my mother did in her past to the men who loved her. Grant deserved more than that.

"She can't make anyone happy until she finds a way to be happy. Right now she has so much resentment in her that she will make anyone who gets too close miserable. Don't let her do that to you."

Grant was quiet for a minute. "She isn't always a bitch. Part of me was falling in love with her for a moment. Then she ended that reminding me how hard she would be to love."

"I love my sister. But you deserve more. Nan isn't whole. Not really. She has too many issues."

"Thank you. I thought this conversation would go a lot differently. I didn't expect you to be worried about me."

"You're my brother. I want what's best for you too. I want you to have what I have. Go find that."

Grant let out a laugh that sounded like he didn't think it was possible. "That's a pretty high order to fill."

BLAIRE

I stepped into the kitchen to see Dean Finlay frying bacon and whistling the tune to one of Slacker Demon's number one hits. I couldn't keep the smile off my face. He turned his head and his gaze met mine. The look on his face wasn't one I ever expected to see on a famous rock star. He reminded me of a father.

"Good morning, sunshine. I'm making you and that grand-baby of mine some breakfast. I did have help but I'm afraid I told Rush something he didn't know and shocked him a bit. He went outside to make a phone call. He'll be back in a few minutes," he said as he forked the bacon and laid each slice out on a paper towel lined plate.

I glanced past him to the windows to see Rush talking on the phone intently. "What did you tell him?" I asked wondering if I should go check on him.

"Grant and Nan have had a thing for awhile now. Nan finally

screwed things up for the last time and it's over. Rush didn't know about it."

My mouth dropped open as his words sank in. Grant and Nan? Really?

"Shocked the hell outta me too. Didn't think that boy was stupid. Guess he learned the hard way, just 'cause it's pretty don't mean it shines."

I looked back outside at Rush. He was standing up and slipping his phone into his pocket. I wondered if he'd called Nan or Grant.

"Why don't you go take a seat over at the table and let me fix you a plate? Do you like orange juice or milk or both? The baby probably needs a little of both."

I shifted my attention back to Dean as he stood there holding a plate with bacon, eggs and a waffle on it. Had he just cooked all that for me?

"Wow, that looks delicious," I replied.

"It is. I make a killer breakfast. Now go sit down and let me feed you."

I bit my bottom lip to keep from grinning like an idiot and walked over and took a seat at the table. Rush opened the door and walked back inside just as his father placed a plate of food in front of me.

"Don't worry about your pretty little fiancée. I got her all fixed up."

Rush smirked at his father then headed over to me. He bent down and placed a kiss on top of my head. "You look beautiful," he whispered.

"Are you okay?" I asked, unable to hold back my concern. I needed to know he wasn't upset about Grant and Nan.

"Yeah, I'm fine. I think Grant has wised up and it'll all be okay."

I frowned. Grant wised up? What did he mean?

"We'll talk about it later. Eat," he said with a wink, and walked over to fix a plate for himself.

Dean put a glass of orange juice and milk in front of me then took the seat to the left of me. He was holding a large cup of coffee in his hands but that was all.

"You aren't going to eat?" I asked, as he drank from the steaming cup.

He shook his head. "Nope. I just drink my breakfast."

Rush put his plate down on the other side of me. He had piled it with everything that was left over. Apparently he was hungry. "Sorry I didn't get to help you finish it but thanks for cooking."

"Glad I got to. It's been awhile since I cooked you breakfast," Dean replied.

I liked seeing Rush with his dad. They appeared normal. I was getting to be a part of his family this way. I doubted I'd ever get this chance with his mom and sister but his dad seemed to accept me.

"Now that I know you can cook, I'm going to volunteer you to help me cook our Thanksgiving dinner," I informed Dean.

Dean grinned. "I would love to. It's been awhile since I've had one of those too. I'm looking forward to spending it with the two of you."

The pleased smile on Rush's face warmed me. "I'm going to go to the grocery store today and buy the rest of our supplies."

"I'll go with you," Rush replied.

"No, you will stay here with your dad. Y'all could go play a round of golf or something. I can pick up what we need by myself. Besides, I think Bethy wants to tag along. She's making the corn casserole and pumpkin pie for tomorrow."

"I refuse to play fucking golf. But spending the day catching up sounds good. We could go over to Destin and catch the new Bond movie. I've been wanting to see it. I'll even take you to lunch."

I could tell by the look on Rush's face he didn't want to go and I knew it was only because he hated to get that far away from me. I reached over and squeezed his hand tightly. "That sounds like fun. Y'all go do that and I'll have time to spend with Bethy."

Rush nodded but I could tell he hadn't wanted to give in.

I took a bite of my eggs and smiled over at Dean. "These are so good. Thank you."

He beamed at me. I was glad he was here. This holiday we wouldn't be completely without our parents.

"Please, Blaire. I am begging you, please," Bethy stood in front of me bouncing on her toes with her hands folded in front of her like she praying. The pleading look in her eyes almost made me laugh.

"Didn't you grow up here? How is it that you've never met Dean before now?" I asked as I took a grocery bag out of the back of the Range Rover.

"I'm the poor folks. You know that! I work for the rich not socialize with them. Come on, I know I'll see him tomorrow but I want to meet him now. While Jace isn't here to see me swoon."

I made a gagging noise. "He's too old to swoon over. Gross!"

"You are kidding me right? Dean Finlay's last girlfriend was like twenty-one. Someone like him never gets too old to swoon over."

I disagreed. Dean was close to fifty years old. He had to be. Why was he dating someone younger than his son? That was disgusting. "You planning on leaving Jace to become one of Dean's notches on his bed post?" I teased and headed for the front door of the beach house.

"Of course not. I just wanna," she stopped and grabbed a bag then scrambled up the steps behind me. "I just wanna meet him. See those eyes and breathe the same air."

This time I did laugh. I couldn't help it. She was cracking me up. "He's a normal guy. He's also Rush's dad and I doubt Rush will want you coming into the house acting like a complete and total fan girl. So you need to get it together before Thanksgiving dinner. It's not a place for you to be swooning over my future father-in-law."

"That is just crazy. You know that right? Just flipping crazy! Having Dean fucking Finlay as your father-in-law. Women around the world want to fuck the man. You're gonna be his family."

I cringed and unlocked the door to the house. Sometimes Bethy could be too much. This was one of those times. "Let's unload the groceries and talk about tomorrow's menu. Then I can tell you all about how I'm leaving this weekend to head to LA with Rush and his father. Nan is causing problems with Kiro."

Bethy hurried inside after me. "You're leaving? This weekend? You can't leave me! Not even for Dean! No!"

At least I had her mind off of humping Dean. I sat my bag down on the counter and turned to look at her. "Rush needs to go and so I'm going with him. Besides, if I don't go I don't think he will. His dad asked him to help deal with Nan."

Bethy pouted and sank down on the bar stool across from me. "This sucks. I don't want you to leave."

The more I thought about it, I didn't want to leave either. But I wasn't letting Rush go to LA without me. I would miss him like crazy. This would also be a chance for me to get to know his dad. We were about to have our own family and I wanted his dad to be a part of that. I had only heard from my dad once since he came by to tell me that he wasn't Nan's father. He had called me a week after he left to tell me he was heading to the Florida Keys to find a boat and live on it. He wanted to be alone. He also told me he loved me.

I tried not to think of my dad much. It only made me sad. I should have told him I wanted him in my life but I hadn't. I'd let him go. Now, looking at the holidays without him, I felt sad. I had found my home but he had lost his.

"Have you heard anything I just said?" Bethy asked, breaking into my thoughts.

I glanced over at her. "I'm sorry. I was thinking about my dad," I admitted. Then I grabbed the can of green beans and started putting it away.

"Oh. You thinking of inviting him?"

It was too late now. I wasn't sure Rush would be okay with it if I did. We hadn't discussed my dad that much. I shook my head and turned to get the box of powdered sugar. "No. Just thinking about him in general. Wondering what he's doing," I replied.

RUSH

My dad was singing in the kitchen while preparing the turkey. I stood back and watched as Blaire mixed something in a bowl and smiled happily. My dad kept trying to get her to sing with him and she would just laugh as she shook her head no. Today was going to be hard on her and I liked seeing her smile.

All week I had debated on telling her I'd invited Abe. He would be here in an hour. I got a text from him when his plane landed. I couldn't decide if surprising her was such a good idea. I wanted to make this special for her. It was our first Thanksgiving together. I knew that the fact it was her first Thanksgiving without her mother was going to overshadow it and I understood that. But if I could make this a good memory, one she would cherish, I would move heaven and earth to make that happen.

"You hiding back there 'cause you're afraid to get your hands dirty, boy?" My dad asked, glancing back over his shoulder and winking at me.

Blaire turned around with a spoon in one hand and a smile on her face. The apron she was wearing had frilly things around the seams and pink polka dots all over it. She was adorable.

I walked over to her and pulled her close so I could kiss those pretty lips of hers.

"We're cooking in here. No time for that stuff," Dean said with a chuckle.

Blaire broke the kiss and pressed her lips together. The twinkle in her eyes let me know she was trying hard not to laugh. I loved seeing her like this. Especially on a day like today. Once again, Blaire was tougher than most men I knew. She continued to blow me away with her strength over and over again.

"Can I help?" I asked, leaning down to press one more kiss to the corner of her mouth.

"Yeah, you can help me get this big ass turkey in the oven without dropping it or burning my damn hand," Dean barked.

Blaire stepped back from me. "Help your dad," she replied, still amused. Good. If Dean could amuse her then he was good for something.

There was a brief knock on the door and then Bethy's voice filled the house. "I'm here!"

"It's about time," Blaire called back.

Bethy walked into the kitchen with Jace following behind her. His hands were full of grocery bags. How we could possibly need more food I wasn't sure.

"Where do I put this?" he asked out of breath.

"Just right there on the counter," Blaire pointed to the only available space in the kitchen.

Jace sat the bag down and let out a sigh of relief then looked at me. "I need a beer and I wanna watch some football."

I opened the fridge and took out two beers and handed one to him. "Come on. Let's get out of the way."

Jace glanced back at Bethy who was standing frozen in her spot staring at my dad. He shook his head and looked back at me. "Yeah, let's get out of here before Bethy goes completely fan girl on your old man."

"Good to see you again too, Jace," Dean called out as we left the kitchen.

"You too, Dean. Please overlook my girl. She's a bit star struck," he replied.

I walked past the living room and the one hundred and three inch flat screen as Jace looked back at it longingly. I knew he wanted to watch a game but I needed to talk to someone about Grant.

We stepped out onto the porch and I sat down on one of the lounge chairs. "Sit. We'll watch a game but I wanted to ask you about something first."

Jace sat down beside me and took a drink of his beer. "You look serious."

"Did you know about Grant and Nan?" I asked, watching him closely. Jace couldn't lie for shit. The widening of his eyes told me he had known. I didn't even wait for his confirmation. "You didn't think telling me was important?" I asked.

Jace put his beer down and let out a frustrated groan. "Shit. I knew you'd be pissed when you found out. I didn't want to be the one to tell you. Besides, you were dealing with losing Blaire and then getting her back. Then her pregnancy. Grant didn't even know I knew. He thought he was keeping it a secret from everyone. We were just more observant than you were at the time. All you could see was Blaire. The rest of us noticed things . . ."

He was right. I had been fighting for my future. I had been focused on getting Blaire back and then protecting her and our baby. I hadn't had time to notice anything or anyone else. Maybe it was best I hadn't known. I hadn't needed any distractions.

"You're right. It's best I didn't know. I'd needed to be focused on Blaire. Not anything else then."

Jace shook his head. "Didn't go down well, though. Nan just leaves destruction in her wake. Grant got real tore up about it but he's dealing with things better now. I think he's gonna move back to Rosemary permanently for awhile. He wants distance from her."

My little sister sure knew how to cause problems. I was getting tired of always bailing her out. I couldn't make it better for Grant though. He knew better when he went into any relationship with her. She didn't do commitments.

The phone in my pocket vibrated and I pulled it out to see a text from Abe. He was here. I prayed that bringing him here was the right thing to do. I wanted today special for Blaire. She'd had enough heartache.

BLAIRE

Rush came walking back into the house with a nervous look in his eyes. He didn't look my way as he headed through the kitchen. I stopped kneading the dough for the biscuits and wiped my hands on the apron before following him. Something was wrong.

I hurried down the hallway and then into the foyer. Rush was opening the front door. Was he leaving? No one had knocked. As the door swung completely open I looked past Rush and saw my father standing there with a small suitcase in one hand and a paper bag in the other. He was thinner and he had a beard. The polished looking man that he had been was gone. He looked like a sea captain now. I couldn't take a deep breath as his eyes met mine over Rush's shoulder. He was here. My daddy was here.

Tears filled my eyes and I started walking towards him. We hadn't spent a holiday together since I was fifteen years old. But this year, he was here. Rush glanced back at me and I understood the look in his eyes earlier now. He didn't want to upset me. He had been trying to surprise me but he hadn't been sure this was the right thing to do.

All the lies and betrayal no longer seemed important as I stared up at my dad's face. He'd suffered too. He still was suffering. Maybe he deserved it. But maybe he had paid his penance. Because right now all I could think about was the man who sang Christmas carols with me as we stuffed the turkey on Thanksgiving, the man who made sure to make a caramel pie because I preferred it over pumpkin pie, and the man who spent hours every Thanksgiving weekend covering our house in Christmas lights. I didn't think about the other. I just remembered all the good.

"Daddy," I said with a tear-clogged voice.

Rush stepped back and allowed him inside. I threw myself in his arms and inhaled the scent that had always reminded me of family, security, and love.

"Hey, Blaire bear," he replied. His voice was thick with emotion. "Happy Thanksgiving."

"Happy Thanksgiving." My voice was muffled in his leather jacket. I wasn't ready to let him go just yet.

"I was worried you wouldn't have your caramel pie. So when Rush called, I figured I better take him up on his offer and make sure my girl got her pie."

A choked sob escaped me and I followed it with a laugh. "I haven't had one of those in a really long time."

"Well, we need to fix that now don't we," he said, with a pat on my back.

I nodded and stepped back from his embrace. "Yeah, we do."

He held up the bag he was holding. "Brought my ingredients."

"Okay," I reached over and took it from him. "You can go put your suitcase in the yellow room if you want to. I'll take this to the kitchen."

Dad nodded his head and then looked over at Rush. "Thank you," he said before turning and heading for the stairs.

I didn't wait until he was completely out of view before I wrapped my arms around Rush's waist and kissed his chest. "I love you," I told him. Because it was more than a thank you. He had done something for me I knew wasn't easy for him. Rush wasn't a fan of my dad but he'd put that aside and brought him here.

"I love you too. More than life," he replied, holding me against him as he kissed the top of my head. "I'm glad this makes you happy. I wasn't sure . . ."

I tilted my head back so I could see his face. "I'll never forget this Thanksgiving. What should have been the hardest holiday I've ever faced isn't so bad now. You make everything better."

Rush flashed me a crooked grin. "Good. I'm trying my hardest to get you so wrapped up in me you never leave."

Laughing, I stood on my tiptoes and pressed my lips against his. "Never. I can't even imagine life without you."

"Mmmmm, you keep that up and we're going back upstairs," he whispered against my mouth. I leaned back and ran my hands up his chest to gently push him back.

"Time for that later. I have a meal to prepare and you have football to watch."

Rush's eyebrows shot up. "Sweet Blaire, I'm not one to sit back and enjoy the action. I prefer to experience the action. Watching football does not compete with getting you naked and under me."

I felt my cheeks flush as the vivid image of Rush on top of me as he moved inside me flashed in my head. Yes, I liked that too. Very much. Rush chuckled and reached over to cup my face and brush his thumb against my cheek.

"You look a little turned on now . . . I can fix that for you. I promise to make it fast so you can get back to cooking," he dropped his voice to a husky whisper.

My breathing hitched and I managed to shake my head no. I had to go cook. My dad had just arrived and Bethy was very likely driving Dean crazy in the kitchen. "I need to get back in there," I replied.

Rush slipped a hand on my waist and tugged me back up against him. His head lowered until his mouth was hovering over my ear. "We can step into that office right there and I'll slip my hand up this cute little dress you're wearing and play with your wet pussy until you have to bite my shoulder to keep from crying out. Won't take long. I don't want my girl needing me. I want her satisfied."

Oh God. I was sure my panties were soaked. It was bad enough that I stayed horny with this pregnancy. Then add Rush and his dirty mouth to it and I was a mess.

"Five minutes," he said before taking a nip at my ear.

I grabbed his arms and held on tight before I melted in a puddle on the floor. "Not now. We can't now. I have to finish in the kitchen and my dad just got here," I said breathlessly.

Rush let out a defeated sigh. "Okay. But damn, I wanted to touch you and feel you come apart on my hand."

"Rush. Please," I said, taking deep calming breaths. "I need some ice water poured down my dress as it is already. Don't make it worse."

With a soft laugh he dropped his hands from me and stepped back. "Fine. Run from me, sweet Blaire. You have five seconds before I decide I don't care what you say."

Moving my legs was going to be difficult but I managed to turn and flee to the kitchen. Rush's laughter grew louder and I couldn't help but laugh too.

RUSH

The turkey had been great and I had to admit, I was impressed Dean could cook like that. Blaire had seemed genuinely happy as she talked with her dad and mine during dinner. She'd even laughed when Bethy had asked my dad to sign her napkin.

Dean came and sat down beside me on the sofa and let out a contented sigh. He had enjoyed himself too. This was the first Thanksgiving I'd actually eaten in my house with family and friends. The first time I'd had turkey, pumpkin pie and corn casserole. Normally my Thanksgivings were spent in Vail. I would eat with friends and get drunk in bars. Nothing memorable. Today had been different. It was a taste of my future with Blaire.

"You got yourself a sweet one," Dean said.

"Yeah, I know."

"She's in there washing dishes with her dad. Figured I'd leave them alone. Give them time together. Shit thing he did to her, but I'm glad they're finding a way to make amends. Abe was a good man once. When I'd heard he was back with your momma I wondered what the hell had happened to him."

I'd betrayed Blaire too. I'd hurt her. But she'd forgiven me. She seemed to be able to do that. I wasn't sure I'd be able to do the same. "I don't deserve her. I'm probably the luckiest sonuvabitch on the planet."

Dean let out a hard laugh. "Glad she makes you feel that way 'cause boy, your life hasn't been an easy one," he paused then shook his head. "I wish I'd done better by you. Kiro's girl, Harlow, has been around lately. Part of the problem with Nan is Harlow. She ain't real happy about Kiro having a daughter he took care of. Kiro might not have been around for Harlow but he made sure she was well taken care of. Her grandmother raised her right. She's a good girl. It's hard to believe she's Kiro's. Poor girl lost her grandmother a few months ago. She's not happy living in LA but she's a little lost right now."

I'd only met Kiro's daughter twice. We were kids and Kiro had brought Harlow home for a visit. I was there too and all I could remember were her big innocent eyes and the way she only whispered when she talked. Then a couple years ago I'd met up with her again while I was visiting Dean. She'd been all grown up but very proper and still very innocent. We had gotten along easy enough that weekend. She stayed at the house most of the time. So had Kiro. It had been the only time I'd ever gone out partying with the band that Kiro had stayed behind. Dean had said he was real protective of Harlow.

I couldn't imagine Nan was handling the existence of Harlow well. Just another thing I had to deal with. "As soon as Blaire is ready we'll leave and I'll handle Nan. She just needs someone who cares about her to talk to her. She's hurt and lost. She has been her entire life."

"I have pie and coffee. Anyone want some?" Blaire asked walking into the room wearing her apron again. Seeing the small baby bump outlined behind it made the caveman instinct to take her and carry her off and protect her pound in my veins.

I stood up and walked over to her. "They can get their own coffee and pie. I wanted to talk to you about something. You've fed and entertained everyone long enough." I told her slipping an arm around her waist.

"Okay, but I don't mind," she replied. I knew she didn't mind. I did. Seeing her all smiling and happy made me want to please her more.

"Just a few minutes," I assured her and led her back to the hallway.

"Rush, what's wrong?" she asked.

I kept my hand on the small of her back and walked us back to the office I'd promised to take her in earlier. No one used this room anymore. I was about to put it to use.

"You were offering dessert in there. I want mine," I told her, closing the door behind me and locking it before backing her against the large leather chair. "Sit down," I growled and Blaire quickly sank down onto the leather.

I knelt down in front of her and slipped that short little dress up her thighs like I'd been fantasizing about all day. She willingly opened her legs for me. The pink silk panties she was wearing had a noticeable wet spot on the crotch. I inhaled and breathed her in. She always smelled so good.

"Rush," she whispered, leaning back in the chair. "We shouldn't be gone long. We have company."

I wish they'd all fucking leave. "I won't take long. I promise. I just need to take care of a little matter," I replied and ran my finger over the wet spot on her panties. "My girl needs some special attention."

Blaire whimpered. I loved that sound. I reached up and took her panties and slid them down her legs. When I got to the backless peep toe heels she was wearing I took off each shoe then pulled her panties off completely dropping them on the floor beside her shoes.

I could smell her arousal now. I put my hands on each of her knees and pressed them further apart so I could look at her pink folds. The little swollen clit was right there begging me to touch it. I glanced up at Blaire. "Lay back," I instructed and she did as was told. Her body trembled and I knew she wanted it just as badly as I wanted to give it to her. "Put that leg up on the arm of the chair and this one of the floor," I said watching as she made herself completely spread open for me.

I positioned myself between her open legs and ran the tip of my nose up the inside of her thigh taking in her scent. Enjoying it and the feel of her leg shaking under my caress. When I got to her needy little spot I ran my finger over it and she cried out then covered her mouth with her hand to smother the sound.

"You ready for me to make this all better?" I asked, pressing my thumb against her clit.

"Oh, God, please, please, Rush, I need you," she begged, lifting her hips so that she was closer to my face.

"You smell fucking amazing," I replied inhaling deeply.

"Please," she cried out desperately.

I didn't want my girl to have to beg so hard. I flicked my tongue out and ran it from just outside her pink puckered untouched hole to the dripping wet swollen one so ready for me. I jammed my tongue into her heated entrance several times as she bucked and muffled her sounds with her own hands. Blaire's taste was unique. It always had been but something was even more desirable about it now that she was pregnant. It was richer and sweeter. I could spend hours tasting her and having her come all over my tongue. It never got old. It was more of an addiction.

"No dessert tastes this fucking perfect," I groaned against her clit before I pulled it into my mouth and sucked on it. I flicked the piercing in my tongue over it several times and the quivering and moaning coming from Blaire told me she was close. So very close. "Shhh, I'm making it feel good. Easy. I'll lick my girl's pussy until she can't stand it anymore. Come in my mouth. I wanna taste it." I knew talking dirty to her would set her off and it did. Blaire let out a strangled cry and her hips lifted as she jerked against my tongue. That addictive taste I couldn't get enough of flooded my mouth and I sucked it up, lapping her until she was moving back and making distressed sounds of pleasure pain.

"Rush no, oh God no. I can't," she moaned moving away as I continued to hold her still and taste every corner of her before sliding my tongue back into her entrance. "Rush, I'm not going to be able to muffle this. I'm about to scream. I can feel another. Oh . . . oh . . . Rush," she jerked and rocked her hips as I held onto her. Her reaction was making me a little crazy. Knowing she was about to go off again so soon was more exciting than I imagined. My cock was already in pain from the swollen unfulfilled head pressing against the zipper of my jeans. If she went off again I was pretty damn sure I was going to mess up my fucking pants.

In one move I stood up and jerked my jeans down then grabbed her hips and slammed into her. "Fuck," I cried out as her tight walls clinched around me. Blaire went off again and this time she wasn't covering her mouth. She was lost in her bliss. Her head was thrown back and her body was bucking wildly under mine as she said my name over and over. The site of her sent me over the edge. I grabbed the back of the chair as I spilled inside her. Each thick burst of my release causing another strangled cry of pleasure from Blaire. She'd raised her legs up to wrap them around my waist at some point but now that she was sated and spent she let them fall back down on the chair. A please smile was on her lips and her eyes were heavy.

"Is it bad that I don't even care if someone heard us? That was too amazing to worry about anything else," she asked.

I lowered myself down until I could kiss her lips. "They shouldn't be in my damn house if they don't want to hear us," I replied.

Blaire giggled. "God, Rush. You make me crazy."

I couldn't keep the grin off my face. "Good."

BLAIRE

Saying goodbye to my dad wasn't as easy as it should be. Having him here helped heal so many wrongs. I followed him outside and down the steps. He had his suitcase in his hand and he was headed back to south Florida where he was living on a boat.

"It's good to see you happy. It'll be easier to sleep at night knowing you're taken care of and well loved. I don't reckon that boy ever expected to be so wrapped around your little finger but he is and I couldn't be happier."

"You'll come back for the wedding and after the baby is born? I want you here."

Dad nodded. "I wouldn't miss that for the world."

I refused to tear up on him. That wasn't fair. He was already all alone. I didn't need to let my emotions confuse him. "Be deciding what you're gonna have him call you. Dean has already said he wants to be Papa Dean. You need to pick a name too."

Dad grinned. I liked seeing him truly excited about something. "I'll think about that and get back to you. Needs to be cooler than Dean's."

I wrapped my arms around his waist and hugged him. "Thank you for coming. I've missed you."

"I've missed you too, Blaire bear, but then that is my fault. I'm thankful Rush called me."

I was too. Rush was at the center of everything good that happened to me. I believed he always would be. Strange considering how it had started out so differently.

"Have a safe flight and call when you get back to let me know you made it okay."

Dad nodded and I stepped back away from him. "I love you," he said with unshed tears glistening in his weary eyes.

"I love you too, Daddy."

He opened the door to the rental car and I stood there as he drove away. This time I wasn't heartbroken. I just hoped that he could find happiness again one day. It was time he did.

The door to the house opened and I turned around to see Rush standing on the front porch looking down at me. I could tell he was worried that I was upset about Dad leaving. I started making my way back to him and he came down the steps to meet me halfway.

"You okay?' he asked the minute he was close enough to touch me.

"Yes. Thank you again for that. It meant more than you could ever know," I told him.

"Whenever you want to see him just tell me. I'll bring him back again. Just say the word."

"I want him here for the wedding and when the baby is born. I want him to get to meet his grandson. He doesn't have anyone but me left. Our son will be his family too."

"Done. I'll have him a plane ticket purchased and ready for the minute we need it."

I just stood there and looked up at Rush. When I'd first laid eyes on him I'd been awed at his beauty. Never had I thought that the moody playboy could have a heart the size of his underneath all that swagger. "What changed you? You're so completely different from that guy I met back in June," I said, smiling at his confused face.

Rush reached out and slipped his hand into my hair and tangled his fingers around the strands. "This sweet, determined, sexy-as-hell blonde walked into my life and gave me a reason to live."

My chest got tight and I started to tell him just how much I loved him again when I felt it . . . the baby.

I reached out and grabbed Rush's arm. "Rush. He's kicking me," I said in amazement. I'd wondered for weeks now if the little flutter in my stomach was him moving. I'd wanted to believe it was. But now I could actually feel him. There was no doubt.

Rush moved his hand from my hair to my stomach and he cradled it with both hands staring down at it with a look of awe. "I can feel him," Rush said in a soft whisper as if he was afraid the baby would stop moving. Instead, at the sound of his voice, the baby kicked again.

"Talk to him, Rush," I said, watching the most beautiful site I'd ever seen. Rush fell down to his knees so that he was closer to my belly.

"Hey you," he said and the baby immediately moved just under Rush's hand. He jerked his head up and looked at me with an excited grin. "He hears me," he said with wonder in his voice.

I nodded. "Yes he does. Talk to him."

"So how is it in there? Is mommy's tummy as cute on the inside as it is on the outside?"

I giggled and he kicked.

"I figured it was. You got lucky. Mommy's beautiful but you'll see that soon enough. We'll be the two luckiest guys on the planet."

He moved again this time with less force.

"You be good in there. We're getting things ready for you out here, enjoy that cozy spot for now."

Rush ran his hands over my tummy and then looked up at me. "He's really in there. He can hear us."

I laughed and nodded. "I thought I'd been feeling him for awhile now but nothing like this."

"God, Blaire, that is amazing," Rush said before pressing a kiss to my stomach and standing up.

"It is, isn't it?" I replied, still marveling at how this was mine. This man in front of me, and the life inside me.

"Tell me when he does it again. I want to feel," Rush said reaching down to take my hand in his.

We walked back up the steps together holding hands.

RUSH

It had been awhile since I'd stepped into my dad's Beverly Hills home. The last time I'd visited I had stayed drunk most of the time and partied with my dad. This would be a very different visit. I wasn't that guy anymore. I set Blaire's suitcase down in the bedroom my dad called mine. It was where I'd always slept when I came to visit him.

"This is just . . . wow," Blaire said walking in behind me. She'd been stopping and taking in the place since we'd walked in the front door. Luckily Nan and Kiro hadn't been here to greet us. I wanted time to get Blaire settled in. The plane ride had been long and I could see the exhaustion on her face.

"You'll learn rock legends are a bit on the showy side. They like to flaunt their success with things," I explained.

"I can see that. They sure have done a good job in flaunting with this place," she said walking over to the bed and then realizing it was too high for her. Glancing over her shoulder she frowned at me. "How the heck am I'm gonna be able to get in this thing?"

I couldn't keep from laughing. She looked so damn perplexed. "I'll get you a little stool."

Blaire grinned and shook her head. "That's just crazy. So, if I wanted to lay down now . . . how might I go about it?"

I walked over to her and put both my hands on her expanding waist then picked her up and put her on the bed. "That way," I replied and sat down beside her before throwing a leg over both of hers and laying her back. "If you didn't look so tired we'd test this thing out," I teased.

She covered her mouth as she yawned and gave me a sleepy smile. "I can stay awake," she assured me and turned her chest towards mine. It was tempting but I knew her body needed rest. I pressed a kiss to her nose. "I'm sure you could, sweet Blaire. But right now all I want to do is massage your feet and calves while you relax and fall asleep."

Her eyes got that pleased glow. "Oh would you? They feel stiff after the flight."

"Go lay your head on the pillow and I'll get rid of these shoes which, by the way, are not exactly walking footwear for a pregnant woman. You should have worn tennis shoes not heels."

Blaire yawned again and settled back on the pillow with a sigh. "I know. I just didn't want to arrive at LAX looking frumpy."

She could never look frumpy. "That would be impossible."

She smiled and closed her eyes as I began rubbing her arch. "You just love me."

"More than life. But that doesn't make me blind. You'd be hot in a potato sack."

She didn't say anything back. Her eyes were closed and her smile still lingered. I put my attention to massaging her tired feet and then worked my way up her calves. By the time I was finished she was breathing slow and evenly. I pulled the blanket over her before leaving to let her rest.

Dean was reclining back on the black leather sectional sofa that took up most of the entertainment room. He had their latest album pumping over the speakers and he was playing Halo on his Xbox with a cigarette hanging out of his mouth.

"While we're here please don't smoke around Blaire," I said as I walked into the room.

Dean glanced over his shoulder and grinned. "I won't. Don't want to hurt the kid."

He pressed pause on his game and threw the remote down on the long sleek red table that sat in front of the sofa then picked up his glass. I didn't have to ask to know it was straight up whiskey.

"Our girl taking a nap?" he asked, propping his feet back up on the table.

The fact he called Blaire "our girl" rubbed me the wrong way. She wasn't anyone's girl but mine. That was the way my dad talked though. He acted like we were a joint thing. He always had. "My girl is asleep. She was exhausted," I replied taking a seat at the other end of the sectional.

Dean just laughed and took a drink of his whiskey then took a drag from his cigarette. "You're a little caveman possessive over her aren't you? Didn't get that from your old man."

I didn't get a lot of things from him but I didn't say that. "I'll do whatever needs to be done to make her happy. But I'll be the one making her happy. Always. Just me."

Dean let out a low whistle and shook his head as he took the cigarette from his lips and flicked his buds into an ashtray. "Tall order to fill. Good luck with that. Women can bitch sometimes, just 'cause they want to. Ain't no one can make a woman happy when she's bitchin'."

This conversation was pointless. He had never had a Blaire in his life. He had no idea what she was like. I was here for a reason and I wanted to address the problem and go home. "Where's Nan?"

Dean sighed and rolled his eyes. "Not here right now, thank the fuck. She's a crazy bitch."

"Where's Kiro?" I asked deciding to ignore his opinion of Nan.

"I'm right fucking here! There's the man! Look at you all fucking grown up and manly. How'd that happen in a few damn months," Kiro's loud voice was unmistakable.

He walked into the room with some girl who looked about my age draped on his arm. Her cleavage was about to pop out of the tied up shirt thing that looked like a corset. She winked at me. Her lashes were obviously fake. No one's lashes were that damn long.

"Came to deal with Nan," I replied looking back at my father who was taking another long drag on his cigarette as he let his eyes roam over the female that Kiro had brought with him. I knew they shared from time to time. That was not the kind of shit I wanted Blaire to be around.

"Holy fuck, I owe you my left damn nut. She's driving me up the fucking wall. Please calm her crazy ass down and help me find a way to talk to her. She always been this insane?"

I knew Nan had her problems but hearing the man that was the main cause behind them talk about her like this pissed me off. I stood up and turned to glare at him. "If she'd had a parent who gave a fucking shit about her maybe she'd have been as normal as Harlow. But she didn't. You left her alone with my mom. NO kid should be subjected to that. At least my father came and got me. Spent time with me. Gave me the feeling of being wanted. You never did that for Nan. She's fucked up because of you." I hadn't meant to go off on him the minute he walked into his house but he'd opened his stupid mouth about my sister.

"It's the boy's sister, Kiro. Be careful about talking shit," Dean warned. He had been talking shit about Nan too but I didn't blame him for her being the way she was.

The girl pressed herself closer to Kiro. "You said this was gonna be fun. I want some fun, baby. You got my pussy all wet in the limo. It's ready to be fucked," she crooned.

This was also something I didn't want Blaire to hear and see. They made sex cheap and dirty. I wanted Blaire to only see it the way it was with the two of us. Not this twisted shit.

"Be a good girl and get naked while I talk to the boy here. Play nice and I might let him kiss that hot slick pussy too."

"Ooooh, good. Two instead of one," she giggled as she pulled the string to her top so that it fell to the floor baring her breasts right there in front of all of us. Again, this was normal behavior when I'd come to visit my dad but things were different now.

"Day—um, she's got them big nipples pierced," my dad said before downing the rest of his whiskey and standing up.

"I'm going back to my room to check on Blaire. I'll talk to you when she's gone," I said with disgust before heading to the door.

"What crawled up his ass? He normally loves enjoying the hot pussy we bring back here," Kiro asked as I left the room.

I didn't waste time getting back to Blaire. She was still curled up on the bed. I slipped off my shoes and went to lie down beside her. Tucking her against me I enjoyed having her close. This was so much more than anything my dad had ever had in his life. The shallowness of his relationships made me feel sorry for him. I knew what he was missing out on. Even with all his success in life he had missed it somehow. So many years lost.

BLAIRE

Rush's mouth trailed kisses down my neck as the shower spray fell from above our heads like it was raining. I wanted one of these showerheads in our house. Both of Rush's hands slipped around my waist and covered my stomach. He had a hard time keeping his hands off my belly since he'd felt the baby kick. It was as if Rush needed to stake his claim regularly. If he wasn't so dang cute when it came to protecting me it would get on my nerves.

Before I could completely enjoy having Rush's body covering my backside and his hands on me, the high-pitched angry scream that I knew belonged to Nan stopped both of us. Rush's body went rigid behind me.

"Nan?" I asked, already knowing the answer.

"Yeah. Guess she found out I was here already," he replied and pressed one more kiss to my neck. "You finish your shower. I need to go deal with this. She and my father do not get along."

I nodded and stood under the warm water as he stepped out of the shower and grabbed one of the large white fluffy towels folded up on a marble pedestal table. I wanted to go with him but he hadn't asked. But then he wouldn't. He was so worried about anyone upsetting me.

A man's deep voice began yelling in response to Nan's screams. Who was that? I had only been around Dean a little but I didn't think the man had ever gotten emotional about anything enough to raise his voice. I turned off the water and grabbed a towel then followed Rush into the bedroom.

"Who else is here?" I asked, as he jerked on a pair of jeans over his naked ass and reached for a tee shirt.

"My guess would be Kiro. Apparently they're having their father daughter bonding," he replied in a frustrated tone.

Kiro. I'd only ever seen pictures of the rock god. But he was here now. In this house . . .

"Just stay in here. This is why we came. So I could deal with her. She's raising hell and Kiro can't manage her. As soon as I get her calm and under control the sooner we can go back to Rosemary."

I nodded and held the towel tightly around me. Rush started for the door then stopped and turned back around. A crooked grin tugged at his lips and he sauntered over to me. His hands slipped into my damp hair and he cupped my face as he gazed down at me. "I just want to stay here with you," he whispered before lowering his mouth to mine.

I grabbed both his arms and held on to him as his mouth

brushed gently against mine before he took a small lick at my bottom lip. I opened my mouth so he could taste more when another shrill scream came from downstairs. Rush pulled back and sighed. "Damn crazy family," he muttered.

"Go deal with it. I'm okay here." A knock at the door surprised me and I pulled the towel tightly against me. Rush stepped in front of me to block anyone's view. "What?" he called out.

I peeked around his back as the door slowly opened. I was mentally preparing myself for Nan to come barging into the room. Instead, a girl about my age stood at the door. She didn't look like anyone I would imagine belonged in this house. Her long brown hair brushed her waist in soft curls and was parted to the side. She had no bangs. It was all one length. Her sultry looking hazel eyes were framed with dark lashes but she wasn't wearing any makeup. The straight-legged shorts she had on hit just at her knee and she was wearing a pale pink blouse that buttoned up the front. It was simple and classy.

"Hello, Harlow," Rush said, surprising me even further. "I'm on my way down. I hear her."

One of the girl's perfectly sculpted eyebrows arched. "I was hoping I could hide up here with you. You're really going down there to deal with that?" The southern twang to her voice startled me. Who was she and why did she have a southern accent? We were in Beverly Hills.

"That's why I'm here. To help the situation," Rush replied.

The girl nodded and then her eyes shifted from Rush to focus on me. "You must be Blaire."

"Yes," I said, glancing up at Rush.

Rush pulled me closer beside him. "Blaire, this is Harlow. She's Kiro's other daughter. Harlow, this is my fiancée, Blaire."

"I know all about Blaire. Dean has filled me in. Do you mind if I stay up here with you, Blaire? Nan isn't a fan of me and I like to stay away from angry people."

"She needs to get dressed and I'm not sure she—"

"Yes, I'd like that. I'll just grab something from my suitcase and slip it on. Won't take but a minute," I replied interrupting Rush. I was normally a good judge of character and I liked Harlow. She seemed almost shy. She was soft spoken and there was no malice in her eyes. She also hadn't ogled Rush when she'd looked at him. That was a major plus for me.

"Are you sure? I was going to have you some food brought up and—"

"The food sounds wonderful. Send some up for Harlow too, please," I said before he could say anything more.

Harlow's laugh startled me and I looked over at her. "I'm sorry. It's just he's being so not like Rush. It's fun to watch him like this."

Yeah. I liked her. "Let me get dressed and you go deal with Nan before she comes looking for you. I don't want to see her just yet."

That seemed to snap Rush out of his determination to keep me bundled up in bed like an invalid. He wouldn't want Nan near me while she was in this mood either. He nodded and headed for the door.

Once he was out the door I motioned for Harlow to come on inside. "I'll just go put on some clothes. Make yourself comfortable."

"Thank you. I've never been in Rush's room before. I typically stay in my room and read. But when Dean told me about you I was curious," she admitted with a shy smile.

"I'm curious about you too. I didn't know Kiro had another daughter. The one I do know isn't very nice. You're nothing like Nan."

Harlow looked sad for a moment. "I was raised very differently from Nan. My Grandmama would have tanned my hide if I'd ever acted the way Nan does. I wasn't allowed to be demanding or throw fits growing up. Grandmama made sure I was well behaved. I think that's why daddy liked to come get me. I didn't get in the way when I came here. I sat in my room and read my books mostly. When he had time for me he'd come get me and we would go to a movie or an amusement park. But other than that my life was with my Grandmama in South Carolina."

So that's why she sounded southern. "I grew up in Alabama. I was wondering about your accent," I admitted.

She smiled. "Most people do. No one expects Kiro's daughter to be a country girl."

I nodded because she was right. They didn't. With a name like Harlow and a famous father I would imagine her to be spoiled and an elitist. She was neither. I pulled out a sundress from my suitcase. I was wearing dresses more often now since my stomach was too big for my jeans.

"I'll be right back," I told her and hurried back to the bathroom to get dressed.

RUSH

Kiro was shirtless and swinging his tattooed arms around with a cigarette between his fingers and a bottle of rum in his other hand. "What the ever loving fuck is your problem? Hell, you got momma issues then go bitch at *motherfucking* Georgianna. Why am I the one being dealt this crazy shit?" Kiro was yelling at Nan when I walked into the game room. A pair of black lace panties were on the pool table but the female I'd left him with a few hours earlier was no where to be seen. Small miracles.

"Rush! Do you hear him? He doesn't care about me. He doesn't care that he ignored me most of my life and do you know he has a daughter? Some uptight bitch that won't even look at me." Nan was still screaming.

I walked over to her and grabbed both her hands. "Take a couple deep breaths, Nan. You gotta calm down so we can all talk. You yelling isn't gonna fix shit."

She glared at me but did as I told her to. I waited until she'd taken two deep breaths before squeezing her hands. "Good. Now, go sit over there on that sofa and don't talk. Let me talk. Okay?"

She frowned but nodded her head and walked over to the white leather sectional sofa that outlined two of the four walls in this room. Once she was seated I turned back around to look at Kiro. He was taking another long swig from the rum. The man needed to stop drinking and eat something. You could see his ribs. His fetish with leather went beyond furniture. He wore it too. The leather pants he had on were hanging on his tattooed hipbones.

"Can't believe you got her to shut up for a whole damn minute," Kiro muttered and put the cigarette back to his lips.

I looked at Nan and shook my head. They were too much alike. They both liked to have the last word.

"She's upset. Please just watch your words and try to remember she's your daughter. The one you abandoned to live with the worst mother a kid could have. Now," I glanced over at Nan. "You can't hate Harlow because he chose to take care of her. You hated Blaire for the same reasons. She never did anything to you but you hated her anyway. There are only two people at fault with the way things ended up. Kiro and Mom. You need to keep your hateful malice geared towards them. Not everyone around them."

"She's made you hate me. You never used to call me hurtful names. I hate her because she took you from me. I can blame her. She took the only family I had that loved me. All you do now is correct me, and talk down to me. You haven't even called me since I left the hospital," she spat and bolted up. "I'm done trying to make you all love me. I shouldn't have to try so hard. I hope you're all happy!" she ran from the room and her heels clicked down the hall and up the steps. I wasn't sure if she was actually leaving or going to throw a fit and see who would follow. I'd followed for too long. I'd helped make her this way.

"Fuck. I needed you around here all along. You can get rid of her with no problem. Damn that was easy," Kiro said as he sank down onto the sofa and propped his feet up crossing them at the ankles. His rum still clinched in his hand and his cigarette hanging out of his mouth. "Sit down and tell me about that girl I ain't met yet. You sure ran outta here fast when Princess dropped her shirt."

The woman's name wasn't Princess. That was what he called all women he screwed. He told me when I was younger that if you called them all the same thing then when you shot your load you wouldn't be caught moaning the wrong name. I'd thought he was a genius back then. Maybe he was in the artist capacity but with women he was an idiot. It was a miracle he still had a dick. He'd stuck it in so many places I'd be worried it was gonna fall off.

"Princess had a fine pussy too. Shoulda seen it. All pink and waxed. I think she even oiled that thing for me."

"Don't want to hear about it. Not why I'm here," I interrupted him before he could go any further.

Kiro laughed and took a pull from his bottle. "She sucked like a damn vacuum too," he said.

"Daddy, please. I don't need the mental images that go along with that," Harlow's voice had me snapping my head around to look for Blaire. She was standing beside Harlow with a pale blue and white striped dress that had long sleeves but the neckline dipped too low showing off her cleavage that was only getting better and better with this pregnancy. It also hit several inches above the knee and she was barefoot.

"Well, I'll be damned, she's one more mouth watering morsel. I'd offer you my lap sweetheart but I think your man just might castrate me if I got too close."

"I'd do more than that," I growled shooting a warning glare at Kiro. Then walked over to Blaire.

"You never sent food up so we came down here looking for something. Everything was quiet in the house so we figured Nan had left," Harlow explained.

Shit. I'd forgotten the food. "I'm sorry, baby. Nan was screaming and I forgot. Come on, let me feed you."

"I already have the new cook, Mr. Branders, fixing us some chicken salad," Harlow replied.

Blaire squeezed my arm. "I'm okay. Stop looking so upset."

Dealing with my family was not what I needed right now. I had Blaire to take care of and our baby. Why had I agreed to come out here? Blaire didn't belong around this kind of lifestyle. The smell of cigarette smoke met my nose and I turned Blaire around and moved her towards the door. "Let's get you out of here. He's smoking," I explained.

"You really making her leave 'cause I'm smoking?" Kiro asked with an amused tone.

I didn't even answer him. I just kept moving Blaire back to the door. I was tempted to tell her not to breathe until I could get her to fresh air. I had to get this Nan shit straightened out and fast. Blaire needed the fresh clean air in Sea Breeze not this nicotine infested place.

"Leave him alone," Harlow scolded Kiro softly.

"Dean wasn't shitting me. The boy has done gone and got himself a pussy," Kiro called out with a hoot of laughter.

I clenched my teeth and kept moving Blaire towards the kitchen.

"He sounds interesting. I never was even properly introduced," Blaire said.

"You don't want to be introduced to him. He's not someone I want near you."

Blaire glanced back at me and frowned. "Why?"

"Because he has no morals. None. At all. And boundaries are a foreign language to him. Women throw themselves at him and he screws them and then moves on to the next one. I don't want him looking at you."

"I really wish I could confirm to him that you do in fact have a penis. A very big and pretty penis," Blaire said in a hushed whisper.

I winced. "Please, just call it big. Don't call it pretty. That hurts its feelings."

Blaire giggled and hurried ahead of me.

BLAIRE

I wasn't sure that a family dinner in this house was a good idea. Rush, however, was determined to find a way to help Nan and Kiro get along. I had spent my day out by the pool. Even though it was the end of November it was still seventy-eight degrees outside. I was used to crazy warm weather in the winter in Alabama but the sun seemed warmer here. Rush had laid out beside me and then he'd taken great measures to rub sunscreen all over my body.

After my shower I felt refreshed and ready to take on this crazy family for Rush's sake. I liked Harlow, at least what little time I'd spent with her. She wasn't kidding about staying locked away in her room. She really rarely ever came out. I almost felt bad for her. It seemed like a lonely life. I wondered what her life in South Carolina had been like. Did she have friends there that she missed?

Rush walked into the bedroom but stopped the moment his eyes landed on me. "No. Blaire, baby, you look amazing. Incredible. But you can't wear that dress too dinner. Your tits are all up there making me want to cancel dinner and get you naked. Then the legs and heels. You can't go to dinner like that. Kiro's a pervert and I'll end up killing him. Please, put on something that shows less cleavage and leg. Hell, wear jeans a sweater and some tennis shoes."

If he didn't look so distraught I would have been pissed. I loved this dress. It made me still feel sexy despite my belly. The bigger the baby got the less attractive I felt. My waistline was quickly disappearing. "None of my jeans fit and I like this dress. It makes me feel pretty."

Rush groaned and walked over to me. "You look fucking gorgeous. Pretty is not the word one would use to describe you in that dress. I need you to look less orgasm-inducing hot and more like my pregnant fiancée. I don't want to listen to Kiro say crude things to you at dinner. I want to focus on getting Nan and him to find some peace."

Okay. "Well when you put it that way I guess I could change," I replied.

"Yes, please. For me," Rush begged.

"Can you unzip me then? I had a hard enough time getting this thing zipped up."

Rush reached around me and pulled the zipper down then pushed it down my shoulders until it fell around my waist. I hadn't been wearing a bra because the back was so low cut and my bare breasts seemed to have caught his attention.

"And wear a bra," he said in a husky whisper. Then lowered his head down to pull one of my nipples into his mouth. The metal on his tongue rubbed against the sensitive flesh and I grabbed his shoulders and held on tightly.

"Rush, we have dinner soon," I reminded him as he slid the dress down over my hips until it hit the floor.

"Right now I fucking don't care," he murmured as he shifted his attention from one nipple to the other. His hand slipped inside the front of my panties and he slid his finger into me with one soft thrust. My knees buckled.

"Please, I . . . please."

"Please, what?" Rush asked, picking me up and putting me on the dressing table behind me. "Spread your legs," he demanded.

I did as I was told. His hand slid down over my mound and his finger began sliding in and out of me in a steady rhythm. Each time he pulled out he slid the wetness on his finger over my clit then pumped back into me. I was very close to an orgasm. Rush seemed to know how to draw them out of me easily.

"Does that feel good? Someone was all wet and ready," he said in my ear and I shivered as his finger slid out this time and moved backwards towards my other entrance. He swirled around it and surprisingly enough it turned me on rather than bothering me. I'd thought it would bother me. The moan that escaped me didn't go unnoticed by Rush.

"You like that?" he asked as his finger gently prodded the entrance. I felt it in my clit. Squeezing my eyes shut I only nodded. "Fuck, baby. I'm not gonna be able to get through this damn dinner thinking about you getting hot and bothered over me playing with your ass."

I didn't want to go to dinner now. I wanted to come.

Rush moved his finger back to my clit and circled it several times then pinched it with his thumb and forefinger while his ring finger slid inside of me. I grabbed his arms and cried out loudly while the orgasm I'd felt building up inside of me erupted.

I went limp in his arms and he held me close to him as his hand slipped out of my panties. He began to lick his fingers one at a time and my stomach quivered as I watched him. A smirk touched his lips as the last finger popped from of his mouth.

"That should hold me over until this nightmare is over. But do me a favor and leave those panties on. I want to go down there knowing I made them all wet."

His words made my breasts ache again. If he didn't stop we were never going to make it down to dinner.

"Put on something that will keep me calm and let's go face the hell that awaits us," Rush whispered as he pulled me up. "Unless you just want to stay in here. I will bring you food if you'd rather skip it."

There was no way I was going to hide up here while he went down there and dealt with Nan. I was going too. Even if I intended to keep my mouth shut I would be there for moral support. "I'm coming with you. Just give me a second. I'm a little breathless and weak."

Rush grinned. "Just the way I like to keep you."

I picked up my discarded dress and threw it at him. Then went to the closet where I had hung up my things and found another dress that fell just above my knees and the neckline was higher. I could wear my knee length boots with this one and it would be cute enough.

I slipped it on and then turned to grab my boots.

"You're wearing boots? Those boots?" Rush asked as I slipped my foot into the first one.

"Yes," I replied.

Rush groaned and shook his head. "Damn boots make a man think of you wearing nothing but those boots."

"Rush. You have got to stop. You think everyone wants to see me naked. In case you haven't noticed I have a stomach that pouches out. No man wants to see me naked . . . except for you."

Both of Rush's eyebrows shot up. "You really think that, don't you?"

"I don't think it, I know it."

Rush let out a defeated sigh. "And that's one of the reasons you're so damn irresistible. Come on, my sweet Blaire. Let's go eat dinner."

RUSH

With Blaire beside me during dinner I wasn't going to be able to focus on Nan. I was going to be protecting Blaire. When Nan had woken up from her coma and she'd found out about the baby she had almost seemed to thaw a little towards Blaire. Then she'd found out Abe wasn't her father. Kiro was.

Nan had been spiraling out of control since then. I understood her desire to have a parent that loved her. I had hated Abe Wynn for years because of the fact my little sister was so broken. But it hadn't been Abe's fault. My mother should have been honest and fucking Kiro should have stepped in like my father had and done something.

Blaire squeezed my hand tightly as we stepped into the dining room. I scanned the room and was relieved that Nan wasn't here yet. I wanted to get Blaire seated and relaxed before my sister showed up.

"You set up this family gathering and you show up late," Kiro drawled as he leaned back in his chair and took in the sight of Blaire. I was beginning to hate the man. For several reasons.

"Nan isn't here yet. We're not late," I replied and walked Blaire to the other end of the table and sat her down beside Dean and I took the chair on the other side of her.

"He's in rare form. Starting hitting the rum early," Dean explained to Blaire. The apologetic look on my dad's face reminded me that he wasn't as heartless as his friend. I knew that already. He hadn't abandoned me. But then Kiro hadn't abandoned Harlow either. However, I wondered if her mother's mother hadn't taken her in if she would have been abandoned. Kiro only supplied the money. Her grandmother had raised her. He'd just shown up with ponies and promises he never kept.

"I'm just being me," Kiro called out from his end of the long table. "You keeping that pretty girl of yours far away from me aren't you?" Kiro said with a laugh. "I'm just looking boy. It isn't like I'm gonna touch her. She's carrying your kid. I stay away from the pregnant ones. I don't want anymore kids blamed on me."

Blaire tensed beside me and I rested my hand on her leg. This wasn't something that should upset her. It was a good thing. Even if I wanted him to stop looking at her.

"Daddy, leave Rush and Blaire alone. Your teasing them just makes everyone uncomfortable," Harlow said. She'd been sitting quietly to the left of Kiro. She rarely talked so I wasn't used to her soft spoken voice. It still amazed me that the man had produced her. She was nothing like Kiro. She was also the only person to make Kiro calm down. Her voice seemed to ease him.

"Alright, darlin. I don't wanna ruin your dinner. I was just funning around."

"No funning," she replied in a gentle command.

Blaire ducked her head beside me. "I like her," she whispered so softly I almost hadn't heard her. I smiled. I hadn't been wrong about Harlow if Blaire liked her. She was genuinely a nice girl. Nan was going to give her hell.

The loud clack of heels hit the marble floor leading into the dining room. I tensed and prepared myself for Nan. She swooped into the room wearing a short ice blue fluffy looking dress with stilettos on and her long red hair was pulled up on her head with curls falling loosely around her face. She had made sure she looked good for this. That was Nan. I watched as her eyes took in everyone at the table with a haughty glance.

The irritated gleam in her eyes as she noticed Blaire was nothing compared to the hateful glare she shot at Harlow. I waited to see if she was going to say something I needed to shut down. Harlow kept her gaze down and she played with the napkin in her lap. The tension in the room was thick and I hated that Nan thought she had to do this to get attention.

"Sit down girl, and stop standing there snarling. We want to eat," Kiro said flippantly and Nan's eyes flashed angrily. She looked at the other seat beside Kiro and then walked past it to sit down on the other side of Dean. The little girl in her was still afraid of rejection. She knew my dad wasn't going to reject her.

"I didn't know you'd brought her," Nan snapped.

Blaire was so tense beside me I wanted to pull her up against me until she relaxed. "Of course I did. She goes where I go."

Nan rolled her eyes. "I miss the old Rush."

"I don't," I replied.

"This is a family matter. You think you could handle just a few moments away from him or are you planning on smothering him the rest of his life?" Nan's hurt was turning into bitterness fast. She wasn't going to take it out on Blaire, though.

I leaned forward on the table and leveled her with my steady gaze. "Do not ever speak to her that way again. If she hadn't agreed to come with me I wouldn't have come. Don't underestimate her importance. She's mine. Respect that."

Nan bristled and sat back in her chair. I hated talking to her this way when I knew she was hurting. But Blaire came first. Always.

"I'm starving. Where's the damn food?" Kiro called out loudly. Two women in their early twenties came hurrying out with trays. Normally there weren't waiters for meals around here. Dean and Kiro weren't big on formal meals. But Dean had called in a catering company to handle tonight's meal. The women had a star struck look in their eyes as they set about putting the appetizers on the table and taking drink orders.

"Look at you," Kiro said as he slid a hand up one of the women's leg.

"Daddy, don't," Harlow whispered.

Kiro let out a hard laugh and winked at the server. "Later."

"God. I can't believe my mother slept with that man," Nan said a little too loudly.

"Don't go there, Nannette," Dean warned beside her. It was too late. I could see the annoyed amusement in Kiro's eyes.

"Why ever not? I'm a fucking rock god, little girl. A fucking. Rock. God." He took a sip of his drink then smiled. "All women want a taste. Your momma was no different."

"Daddy, please," Harlow said, reaching over and touching his arm lightly.

"My mother was too young to know better," Nan shot back.

"She wasn't that young. She was just trying her damnedest to sleep with every one of us. I think she can officially claim the title of 'has fucked all of Slacker Demon' and that's not an easy title. Dean is more picky than most."

Nan's face paled and I knew I needed to step in before this got out of hand. "Thanks Kiro, for making sure we were aware of our mother's sexual habits when she was younger. Now, could we move on from that and try to all get along."

Kiro nodded. "Of course. Let's eat some of this shit."

The servers quickly started walking around the table with the trays of food and asking us what we wanted. Blaire had turned down most all of the appetizers. She had only taken a slice of bread.

"Why aren't you eating more than that?" I asked concerned.

She leaned into me so no one would hear her. "Because I can't eat raw meats or cheeses with unpasteurized milk while I'm pregnant."

Shit. Something else I didn't know. I pushed my chair back and headed for the kitchen. They were going to make her something she could eat.

BLAIRE

I didn't have to ask Rush what he was doing. I already knew. He would be back with food I could eat. If I wasn't so hungry I would try and stop him but I really did want to eat more than bread.

"You've turned my brother into your bitch. It's pathetic," Nan hissed across the table.

"Claws in, Nan. Blaire is pregnant and needs to eat. Rush is taking care of what's his," Dean replied before throwing back a raw oyster off its shell into his open mouth.

"Do you not understand what birth control is? Or was that your plan all along. Hook him with a baby?"

It was very likely that the rest of my life I would have to deal with this kind of attitude from Nan. Getting upset and backing away from it wasn't going to be a life choice for me. Granted I didn't intend to stick a gun in her face again, but I wasn't going to just let her talk to me like that because she was Rush's sister.

"I realize you're hurt and angry. But I've done nothing to you. So, please, back off."

Dean chuckled beside me. Nan's eyes only shone brighter. Great. I'd done nothing but piss her off more.

"You listen to me, you little bitch. No matter what you think you have, you don't. I'm his sister. I'm his blood. He will choose me if it comes down to it. So don't you dare threaten me."

As much as I wanted to go back upstairs to Rush's room and hide away from all this, I knew it would only make her worse. I had to show her I wasn't backing down.

"This isn't a competition. You're his sister. I'm the mother of his child. He doesn't have to just love one of us, Nan. That's childish and insecure to think that way. Rush is here because he loves you and he wants to help you. Don't slap him in the face by treating me this way."

Nan opened her mouth and snapped it closed again. Her jaw was flexing from all the teeth grinding she was doing.

"Thata girl, Blaire," Kiro called out and the pain that flashed in Nan's eyes made me feel sorry for her. I knew what it felt like to have a father not want you. But I also knew what it felt like to have a father who adored you. She didn't.

"I don't know why I even try. No one accepts me here. Rush was all I had and now he has attached himself to you and you hate me," she screeched as she stood up and threw her napkin on the table.

"You took Rush," she pointed a finger at me then she swung

her attention to Harlow. "And you, you have my father's love. I have nothing." She spun around and ran from the room.

Rush walked in just as her heels clacked loudly on the floor and he looked at Kiro. The anger on his face was evident. "What did you do? I was only gone for five minutes."

Kiro shrugged and pointed at me. "Don't look at me. It was your woman that sent her running."

Rush's anger turned to confusion as he shifted his gaze to me. "Blaire? What happened?"

I shook my head. "She was accusing me of things and I just told her the truth."

Rush let out a sigh and took off after his sister.

I sat there wondering if I should leave too. Or if I was supposed to stay here. My bread was forgotten on my plate and my stomach was now in knots.

"This family dinner is slowly dwindling. Anyone else want to run off before we have our salad?" Kiro asked in a jovial tone. How he could be making jokes after what had just happened I didn't understand.

Dean reached over and squeezed my arm. "He'll be back. Sometimes Nan just needs Rush. He knows that."

Unfortunately I knew that too.

Rush wasn't back by the time dinner was over. Kiro was now completely groping the server's bottom underneath her dress. Harlow was ignoring it and finishing her wine silently. Dean had his attention on the other server. I was more than positive the two women were on the menu for both men. The one Dean was looking at kept giggling and finding reasons to walk over to him. Luckily he wasn't going for any body parts yet. I was more than ready to get up and leave.

"I think it might be time for you and Blaire to go on up to bed," Kiro said to Harlow without looking at her. He was focused on the server's boobs and his hand was still up her skirt.

"I completely agree," Harlow replied standing up and looking over at me with an apologetic smile.

I stood up and started to thank Kiro and Dean for dinner when I noticed Dean's hand was now between the other server's legs. I decided to hurry out behind Harlow.

"I'm sorry you had to witness that. Dad's drinking more now that Nan is raising hell. When he drinks he . . . uh . . . requires a lot of women."

In other words he screwed around more often. I nodded. However what was Dean's problem? Just horny rock legend used to getting what he wanted I guess.

"I thought Rush would be back by now," I replied wanting to change the subject.

Harlow nodded. "Yeah me too. Nan can be a handful, I'm realizing."

Handful was a kind word for Nan. I was thinking more along the lines of "bitch".

"She hates me. I guess I need to accept it and learn to live with it. I just don't like the spot it puts Rush in."

A loud squeal and then a moan came from the dinning room. Harlow made a gagging noise. "Ugh, come on. We can take the elevator instead of the stairs. It will drown out the noise."

"Are they just . . . doing it in the dining room?" I asked, amazed at the lack of privacy and the fact the other catering staff could hear them in the kitchen.

"They will do it anywhere. Trust me. You don't want to know what I've seen over the years. I think it's the reason I'm still a virgin. Well, that and the fact I'm too shy around guys."

It was a miracle that Harlow was as innocent as she was with this kind of behavior from her father. "I was a virgin until Rush. Sometimes it's best to wait until the right guy comes along."

Harlow smiled and nodded. "Yeah. But then there is the chance that will never happen. I don't socialize much. My life here is very private. I've always hated sex because of what I've seen it do to my dad. But lately I wonder if maybe I just need to see it in a different light. You and Rush seem happy together."

I felt sad for her. She'd grown up with her grandmother apparently very overprotected then only seen the other side of the spectrum from Kiro's life. She had to be very confused. "Did you date in South Carolina?" I asked.

She shrugged. "Not much. My Grandmama wasn't a fan of me dating. She said it only led to sex. I was to wait until I got married to have sex. It said so in her Bible. But if I didn't date how was I supposed to get married?" Harlow let out a soft laugh. "Didn't matter though. I never could find my words when a guy I was attracted to was around me. I became embarrassingly shy and awkward. I'm getting better with age I think."

Harlow was a classic beauty. She was elegant and perfect. It was hard to believe she hadn't dated much.

"I'm going to go on up to my room. I have a book to finish. Recently I've found indie authors on my Kindle and I'm slightly addicted."

"Indie?" I asked.

Harlow nodded. "Self published ebooks. I've found some diamonds in the rough."

I might need to get a Kindle. "Enjoy then," I replied and headed up to Rush's room.

RUSH

Nan was a sobbing mess. As mean as she was, my heart broke for her. She was still my little sister and she had been done wrong. By both her parents. I had tried all my life to be the one person she could count on but I hadn't been enough. She needed to feel loved and accepted by one of her lousy excuses for parents.

"She hates me," Nan sniffed and hiccupped. "Right there in front of Kiro, she made me look like a fool. She didn't even care that I'm trying to find a way to get him to want me."

I was sure that Nan had pushed Blaire to say the things that she did but I didn't point that out. I was only now, after an hour, getting Nan to calm down enough to talk to me. She needed someone right now and I was pretty sure I was the only person on the planet that cared about her problems.

"I know you love her, but she's mean. She's cold and mean. You remember when she pointed that gun at me," Nan sniffled and wiped at her tear soaked face.

"That was a little different. Mom and Abe had just ripped her world out from under her. She was upset and you were taunting her."

Nan let out a hard laugh. "You will always stick up for her. Even if she made fun of me and my need to have a parent that wants me right there in front of everyone. In front of Harlow. Dean. Kiro. She doesn't care about my feelings."

Blaire was pregnant and her emotions were harder for her to control. However, I needed to talk to her about just being quiet around Nan. The sooner I got Nan and Kiro on good terms we could leave. I didn't like having to juggle Blaire and my sister. It was too much.

"She shouldn't have said what she did. Although, you shouldn't have said anything to her either."

"I was just reminding her that you loved me too. She was glaring at me so hatefully."

Blaire had many reasons to hate Nan. I knew that. I just wish she'd learn to let that all go. When she had insisted we come here I'd thought it was her way of forgiving Nan. Looked like I was wrong.

"I'll deal with Blaire. This won't happen again. But you need to start finding ways to let go of this bitterness, Nan. I can't help you if you keep acting like this in front of Kiro. He is used to dealing with Harlow. Not you. Harlow is quiet and keeps to herself. That's all Kiro will put up with and I am sure as a child she figured that out fast. You need to realize Kiro won't accept you for you. He is spoiled and selfish. He's a legend. People adore him and he thrives off of it."

"I hate my life. I . . . I think sometimes that it would be easier on everyone if I just ended it."

I felt a sharp ache in my chest and I reached over and pulled her into my arms. "You can't do that because I love you. I want you around. You need a chance to find happiness, Nan. Don't do this to yourself. And don't ever, and I mean EVER, say something like that again."

She nodded against my chest and began to cry softly. I wondered if my wounded sister would ever be healed.

It was several hours later before I got back to the house. Nan was back at her hotel. She refused to stay in the house with Kiro and Harlow. I had texted Blaire twice and I'd heard nothing from her. I was worried. I kept telling myself that she was asleep.

I hurried up to our room and opened the door to find her curled up on the bed asleep. She was still wearing her dress and she looked cold. I walked over to her and started to undress her gently. I didn't want to wake her but I also didn't want her to be uncomfortable while she slept.

Once I had her undressed I pulled back the covers and tucked her in. I couldn't believe she'd said something hurtful to Nan. But then Nan had been adamant that Blaire had lashed out at her. It was probably the pregnancy hormones. I bent down and kissed Blaire's head before standing up and heading to go get a shower. We'd not even been here one day and I was already stressed and ready to leave.

The banging on the door started after my head hit the pillow. Or at least it felt like it. Blaire stirred in my arms and I noticed the sun pouring in through the windows. Maybe I had gotten some sleep.

"Who's that?" Blaire asked in a sleepy whisper.

I wasn't sure, but I hadn't wanted Blaire woken up like this. I was sure she'd sat up late waiting on me. "Not sure. Stay here," I replied and kissed her head before getting out of the bed and pulling on my discarded jeans.

I jerked open the bedroom door to find my dad looking hung over and pissed. "You got shit to deal with. Whatever the fuck you said to Nan last night didn't help. Her ass is moving in." Dean snarled.

That was a step in the right direction. She needed a chance to warm up to Kiro. This would be good for them. "Then my talk did help. It's time Kiro accepts her and makes up for lost time."

Dean let out a hard laugh. "That won't happen, Rush. You're blowing smoke up her ass if that's what you're telling her. Kiro is Kiro. He ain't a fucking daddy figure and that's what she wants."

Maybe. But I had to at least help her try.

"Just get downstairs and help before all hell breaks loose," Dean said before turning and stalking off.

I closed the door before turning back to Blaire. She was sitting up in bed with her hair messy from sleep and the sheet pulled up to her bare chest. What I really wanted was to crawl back in bed with her and forget this bullshit with Nan.

"I'm sorry," I told her as I walked back over to the bed.

She frowned. "When did you get back last night?"

"Late. Nan was difficult."

Blaire nodded stiffly then dropped her gaze from mine. I went over to her side of the bed and sat down beside her then slipped a finger under her chin and tilted her head up to look at me. "Hey, what's wrong?"

She let out a weary sigh. "You could have called. I waited for you to call. I fell asleep worried about you."

"I did call," I assured her. "You didn't answer.

Blaire reached for her phone and looked down at it. "You called me after eleven. I had fallen asleep by that time. I meant you could have called sooner than that."

She was right. I should have. Damn Nan and Kiro. I was not going to put Blaire second to anyone else again. I had sworn she came first and I meant it. Yet last night I'd let her down.

BLAIRE

I was trying very hard not to sound like a baby but I was upset.

"I should have called you sooner. I'm sorry. Nan started threatening to off herself and I panicked. I was in big brother mode."

He was always in big brother mode with Nan. Coming here I knew I was in for a lot of Nan, but it was harder than I imagined. Especially after the way she'd treated me last night. I didn't believe for a minute that she'd kill herself.

"She's manipulating you. I hate to see her do that."

Rush stood up and ran his hand through his hair and walked over to the window. He didn't agree with me. I could tell by the stiff way he was holding his shoulders. He looked defensive. "She's upset and hurt. I know she's been a bitch to you in the past but right now I need you. For me, could you not say hurtful things to her? I'm really worried about her mental stability at the moment."

Hurtful things? I hadn't said anything to Nan. Did he think I was going to? "I was the one who said we should come. I understand she needs your help. Why would you think that I would say hurtful things to her?" I asked standing up.

Rush let his head fall back and he closed his eyes tightly like he really didn't want to be having this conversation. Something was wrong.

"I know what you said to her last night at the table. She told me. And yeah, you have every right to say those things to her but right now I just need you not to. The sooner I can fix this the sooner we head back to Rosemary and leave this nightmare."

"What did I say to her last night at the table? I'm not following you," I replied feeling a sick knot in my stomach. Was Nan lying on me? She was the one who had said hurtful things at the table. Not me.

"She feels like you made fun of her. Just . . . it's probably best if you just don't talk to her."

I sat back down on the bed and let last night's conversations run through my head. How did she feel like I'd made fun of her? She'd attacked me.

A soft knock on the door interrupted what I was about to say and Rush let out a frustrated growl before stalking over to open it.

"Sorry. I don't want to disturb y'all but Nan is demanding to know what room is Daddy's. She doesn't need to wake him up. That would be bad," Harlow's soft spoken voice sounded anxious.

"Shit," Rush muttered. He glanced back at me. "I'm sorry.

I'll be back in a few minutes. Just go back to bed and get some rest. I won't let anyone else disturb you."

Once the door was closed I let the tears fall. When I'd told him to come and deal with Nan, I'd thought this would be easier. I had hoped after her accident and her comment about being a part of the baby's life that she'd be more manageable. I was wrong. Coming here had been a bad idea.

My stomach cramped and I froze. I sat still and waited for the baby to kick and reassure me everything was okay. Nothing happened. I put both my hands on my stomach and the cramp came again. Wincing, I tried to calm my heart as it started to race. Something was wrong. A wave of nausea hit me and I laid back and closed my eyes. Maybe I'd gotten up too quick this morning. I needed to start being more careful. All the high-strung tension in this house was getting to me.

I closed my eyes and took slow deep breaths. No more cramps came and I felt a soft kick against my hand. With that little bit of reassurance I drifted off to sleep.

When I opened my eyes the sun had moved, and by the way it was shining brightly through the windows it had to be after lunch. I reached for my phone and checked the time. It was one. I must have been more tired than I thought.

I rolled over to get up and a tray of food was sitting on a small table beside the bed. I wrapped the sheet around me and went over to it. Picking up the small note with Rush's familiar scrawl on it I smiled.

I'm sorry about this morning. You were exhausted and I unloaded on you. None of this is your fault. I just want to get it all over with and get you back home. Eat something. I'm going to go see if I can't talk to Kiro.

I love you more than life,

Rush.

I picked up the silver cover that had been protecting my plate to find fresh strawberries and cream, salmon and a slice of toast. My stomach still wasn't feeling that great so I decided to stay away from the salmon but I took a strawberry and dipped it into the cream before taking a bite. The sweet taste hit my tongue and I felt better. Sitting on the edge of the bed I finished all the strawberries and toast before getting up and having a shower.

RUSH

It was abnormally warm for the end of November. I had put on shorts and a tee shirt and come outside to enjoy the heat of the California sunshine.

Blaire still hadn't come out of the room. If she wasn't up soon I was going to get her a new plate of food and go feed her myself. I was glad she was getting sleep but she needed to eat too. Harlow had said she didn't think Blaire ate much at dinner last night. I should have stayed with her and gone after Nan once I had Blaire tucked away in bed.

If my over dramatic sister wasn't so damn volatile I wouldn't be trying to help her. I just wouldn't be able to live with myself if I ignored her and something happened to her. As much of a pain in the ass as she was, she was still my sister. I still saw the little girl with piggy tails smiling up at me with a toothless grin. She'd been mine when we were growing up. No one else took care of her. It was hard for me to forget that.

"Where's that girl of yours?" Kiro asked as he sauntered out to the back patio where I'd decided to hide from Nan.

"She's sleeping," I replied, glad to see Kiro was outside smoking instead of inside.

"She's a sweet thing. Reminds me of my Harlow," he said, before sticking the cigarette he was holding back between his lips.

"Yeah. She's pretty damn perfect," I agreed.

"You need to protect her a little more from Nan. She was spilling venom all over her last night. Your girl handled it well. I was damn impressed. But you need to take better care of her," he drawled then flicked ashes from his cigarette before turning and walking back to the house.

I started to ask him what he was talking about when Nan came barreling out of the door with a bikini and a pair of stilettos on her feet.

"What're you doing, girl?" Kiro asked her in an annoyed tone.

"Going to get some sun. Why? You want to join me? Maybe talk to me?" Nan spat out hatefully. I wanted to shake her and ask her why she had to be so damn difficult.

"No. I wanna know when you're gonna move your ass outta my house. You keep stirring up drama. Harlow won't even come out of her damn room. It's time you go harass your momma for awhile and leave me in peace." I winced at the sight of the pain in Nan's eyes. Damn Kiro was heartless.

"Why am I even trying? You don't want to know me. You

don't care to know me. You have Harlow and that's all you want. I'm nothing to you." Nan screamed.

"Harlow isn't a mean bitch, Nan. Try being a normal human and I just might want to get to know you. I didn't stay with your momma for a reason, girl. Guess what the reason was," he snarled and pushed past her and into the house.

Nan's eyes looked empty as she stood there staring at the door. Dammit. I stood up and went over to her. She noticed me and shook her head. "No. I don't want you either. You hate me too. You picked her. Everyone picks someone else. No one wants me," Nan cried and spun around and took off running back into the house.

I stopped at the door and listened as her heels clicked loudly on the floor until they faded away. I would have to go and talk to her but I was going to give her time to calm down. She needed some alone time.

"That didn't sound good," Blaire said, breaking into my thoughts. I turned to see her walking down the stairs. Her long blonde hair was pulled up and she was wearing a light blue swimsuit with a white see through cover up that hung off her shoulder and hit at mid thigh. Her eyes looked rested but the worried frown on her face I knew was from what she'd just heard.

"Yeah, it was brutal," I replied, closing the distance between us and pulling her to me before I kissed those pink full lips. I didn't like seeing her frown so much. She slipped her arms around my waist and opened her mouth to me. I tasted the minty flavor of her toothpaste and enjoyed the silky warmth of her mouth.

She moved her soft lips over mine and a soft moan escaped her mouth. Taking her back upstairs to the bedroom was sounding good. She started to pull back and I gazed down into her heavy lidded eyes. She was smiling contentedly. "Harlow said it was warm today. I thought I'd come get some sunshine. I've been inside too much," she said.

She needed fresh air. "I think that's a good idea. Why don't you go lay down on one of the lounge chairs and I'll rub your feet."

Her eyes twinkled with excitement and I almost laughed. She loved having her feet rubbed lately. I knew it was because she was carrying more weight with the baby and she wasn't used to it. "That sounds wonderful," she agreed and hurried over to the closest lounge chair to get settled down.

My phone started ringing in my pocket and I started to ignore it. Blaire looked up at me as I stood over her. "Aren't you gonna answer it?" she asked.

I slipped my hand into my pocket and saw Nan's number flashing on the screen. I should ignore it. This couldn't be good. I wanted time with Blaire. I wanted to rub her feet and watch the sexy little faces she made while I did it.

"Just answer it, Rush. If you don't, you'll worry," she said.

Muttering a curse I clicked answer and held it to my ear. Before I could say hello Nan's loud sobs greeted me.

"Don't come after me. I told you last night I wanted to end it, and I do. This is it. Everyone hates me and I'm done. Goodbye, Rush," she cried into the phone before ending the call.

"Fuck," I growled, stuffing my phone back into my pocket. I had to go after her. I wanted to believe Blaire was right and Nan wouldn't hurt herself but I couldn't just assume this. "She's threatening to kill herself again," I said looking down at Blaire and the disappointed look on her face. I was letting her down again. I hated this. I wish we'd never come but then I also would never be able to forgive myself if something happened to Nan.

"Go on. It's okay. She needs you so she's acting out to get your attention," Blaire replied. Her words made sense. She was probably right.

"We don't know that she's not really going to try something. I can't just believe this is an empty threat."

"I know that."

"I'm all she has, Blaire," I snapped not meaning to. I wasn't mad at Blaire. I was mad that she was so damn understanding and she didn't have to be. I was mad that she kept being put on hold for my family. I hated that she just let me go every time without making me feel guilty. I hated all of this.

"I know," she replied again. This time I could hear the hurt in her voice and I hated myself for putting it there.

"I'm sorry, I just—"

"You just need to go check on your sister. I understand," Blaire finished for me. The hard tone in her voice worried me but we didn't have time to deal with this right now. The longer

I stood here the worse this was going to get. I'd make this up to her later today. I was also going to threaten to check Nan into a mental place until she stopped threatening to off herself. Then we were going back to Rosemary. I wanted my life back.

BLAIRE

Over the next few days things went from tense to bad to worse. Rush hardly stayed at the mansion. When he did it was short lived. Nan and Kiro always fought and she went running off. Rush was right behind her.

I knew this was the reason we had come here but I hadn't expected this. Nan was really more of an immature child than I realized. Kiro was an ass. Harlow saw it and she dealt with it. She wasn't storming around the house yelling about being unloved. She mostly stayed tucked away in her room and read. Every once and awhile she would come outside with me when it was warm enough.

I missed Rush. I missed seeing him smile. He wasn't doing much of that anymore. I had mentioned last night that maybe he needed to give Nan some room to pitch a fit and let her see that he wasn't going to come running. See how she handled it. He'd gotten frustrated with me. "She's threatening to kill herself, Blaire. I can't ignore that. I don't believe she'd do it either, but I still can't ignore it. Someone has to give a shit. That someone is me. No one else does."

I hadn't said anything more after that. He didn't want to listen to me and I didn't want to be snapped at. It was wearing on me. The whole situation was.

I was beginning to understand why Harlow hid away. I'd walked in on Kiro screwing some girl that looked my age twice now. Not a mental picture I wanted. He just did it wherever he pleased. I'd learned to stay the heck away from the game room. That pool table was not used for pool.

A knock on my door broke into my thoughts and for once I was glad. I didn't want to think about the distance between me and Rush right now. It made me tense. Harlow stuck her head in the room. "Want to go out to the pool with me? Dad isn't home so no sexcapades are going on out there," she said with a shy smile.

We had also walked out on Kiro naked in the pool with not one but two girls. That had been awkward. He'd laughed so loudly I was sure his neighbors could hear him. Instead of being embarrassed or ashamed of his behavior he thought he was hilarious.

"Sounds good. I'll get on my swimsuit and meet you out there," I told her. Harlow was the only good thing about this place. I was ready to go back to Rosemary and I was ready to have my Rush back instead of this angry uptight one that had taken his place. But I was going to miss Harlow.

I quickly changed into my swimsuit and pulled my cover-up on before heading down to the pool. It was an elaborate piece of work. The waterfalls and water fountain in the middle of it were just the icing. The detail and thought that had been put into this pool made it truly look like something out of an exotic rainforest somewhere. It was soothing just to look at.

Harlow was sitting on a lounger reading from her ereader when I got down there. I took the seat beside her and stretched out my legs. Today was the warmest day we had had so far. It was eighty degrees. Crazy considering it was two days until December.

I started to ask Harlow about how they celebrated the holidays when something stopped me.

The cramping was back. I pulled my knees up and cradled my stomach trying real hard not to cry. I had wanted to tell Rush about this after the last time but before I'd had a chance he'd left with Nan again.

"Blaire? Are you okay?" Harlow asked from beside me.

"I'm not sure," I replied honestly. A tear slipped through and I hated that she was about to see me like this. I wanted to go home.

Harlow moved over and sat down on the edge of my lounger and studied me. "Are you hurting?" she asked.

I just nodded. Harlow frowned and glanced around. "Where is Rush?"

"Gone to check on Nan," I replied as my stomach cramped up again and I winced.

Harlow stood up. "I don't think pregnant women are supposed to wince and cry from pain. We need to go have you checked on. I can drive you to my doctor. He's a real big fan of Daddy's so he'll see you without an appointment. I'll call his office on our way."

I didn't want to be the one overreacting. So having Harlow do it for me made the decision easier. I nodded and let her take my hand and help me up. "I need to go change clothes first," I said, looking down at the swimsuit and cover up I had just put on.

"You go change and I will too then I'll go get my car and pull it around to the front entrance. I can call my doctor on our way."

"Thank you," I replied before heading inside and up to Rush's room. I thought about calling Rush but changed my mind. He already had one female needing him. This may be nothing more than gas for all I knew. I would call him if the doctor thought I should. No reason to put more stress on him.

The little voice in my head whispered what I didn't want to admit to myself. "*You're afraid you and the baby won't come first. You don't want him to have to choose.*"

I pushed the thought away and slipped off my swimsuit and slipped on a pair of panties and then pulled a sundress on before quickly heading back downstairs. I would feel better after a doctor told me I was okay. Just as I reached the bottom stair another pang hit me and I had to grab the railing to hold myself up. The cramping made me whimper.

"You okay?" the concerned tone of Dean's voice surprised me.

I forced a smile and nodded. "Yeah, I'm okay. I'm just going to get checked out at Harlow's OBGYN. I'll be back soon. Tell Rush I'll call him if I need to."

"Where's Rush at?" Dean called out after me as I made my way to the door.

"With Nan," I replied then opened the door and went to get in Harlow's convertible light blue Audi.

Harlow hadn't been wrong when she said that her doctor would see me right away. We had arrived and the nurse had ushered me back without asking me to fill out paperwork or even sign in.

"I'll wait out here," Harlow told me.

I was glad she wasn't going to come back with me. I liked Harlow but we weren't close enough for her to accompany me back to an examination room just yet.

"Go ahead and take off your bottoms. You can leave your top on. And cover up with the blanket on the table. The doctor will be in in just a moment." The lady informed me. I nodded and thanked her. Once the door was closed behind her I went into the changing room and slipped my bottoms off.

The red streak in my panties made me pause and take a deep breath. The terror slowly starting to invade my thoughts made breathing difficult. I stood there staring down at my panties wondering if this was normal. If this could be okay. I should have called Rush. I took a moment to pray. I didn't do it often but right now I needed someone to protect my baby.

After my silent plea, I stepped out of the dressing room and went over to the table and covered up my bare bottom half. A swift knock on the door then a pause before it opened made me marginally feel better. I was going to have help. This doctor would know what to do. I hoped. A man much younger than I expected walked in followed by the nurse who had brought me to the room.

"Miss Wynn, I'm Doctor Sheridan. Harlow told me that you're experiencing cramps and you're a long way from your doctor in Florida."

I nodded. "Yes, sir. I'm also bleeding a little," the words came out in a choked sob I hadn't been expecting.

"There now, this could be something as simple as dehydration. Don't worry, it won't help things," he said as he took his seat and had me slip my feet up into the stirrups. "What are you doing so far away from home?" he asked as he started to examine me.

"My fiancé and I are here visiting his father," I explained and left it at that. No reason to tell the man the real reason we were here.

"How do you know Harlow?" He asked.

"My fiancé's father is Dean Finlay," I said, figuring if the man was a fan of Kiro he'd be able to figure that out easy enough.

He paused. "Really? So this baby we're checking on in here is Dean Finlay's grandchild?"

I nodded and wished he'd stop asking so many questions and get on with the exam. I needed to know my baby was okay. He seemed to get more serious about his examination.

"I don't want to alarm you Miss Wynn, but we need to do an ultrasound to check the baby and then I want to monitor you and the baby for a couple of hours here in the office. This happens often. I am just taking precautions and making sure all is well. I also want you to drink some fluids for me. Melanie will bring you something to drink once we get finished with the ultrasound. We have a room in the back just for this. It has a comfortable bed. Melanie will dim the lights and play relaxing music while you rest.

He wasn't admitting me to the hospital. This was a good thing . . . right? I managed to nod again.

"I'll have Melanie go tell Harlow what we're doing in case she wants to go do something else until you call her. Is that alright with you?" he asked.

I had forgotten about Harlow. "Yes, of course. Tell her I said to leave. I'll let her know when to come back. I don't want her sitting here all that time."

The doctor nodded and headed out the door. The nurse who I assumed was Melanie helped me up. "Go get your bottoms back on then I'll take you to get the ultrasound."

RUSH

By the time I got to Nan's hotel I was pissed. I had left Blaire upset and it was all Nan's fucking fault. If she wasn't so damn selfish, I wouldn't even be here. I needed to tell her that she had to grow up and deal. I was done. I couldn't keep on doing this. She had to figure this out. I was her crutch.

I knocked on the door to her hotel room and waited. I'd checked with the doorman and Nan had returned about fifteen minutes ago so I knew she was here. I waited a few minutes then knocked again and got nothing. More damn games. I started pounding on the door harder. "Nannette, open this door," I called out.

A bellman paused when he saw me beating on Nan's door. "My sister's in here and she isn't answering. I'm worried about her," I lied. "Could you open the door?"

The man still didn't look too sure about me. I could tell by the look on his face he was close to calling security. Nan would love that. I reached in my back pocket and pulled out my wallet. "Check my license. I'm Rush Finlay. My sister Nannette is in that room. Having me escorted out is a really bad idea."

"Yes sir," the bellman replied. He had recognized my last name. In LA that happened a hell of a lot more than it did in Florida.

He had the door opened and I was stalking inside the suite getting ready to yell at Nan for being a child when I saw her crumpled body on the sofa. She was lying there in an unnatural position. I ran over to her and felt for a pulse, finding a weak one against my fingers. I wanted to weep from relief. "I need paramedics, NOW," I roared as the bellman stood at the door gapping at Nan.

"Yes, sir," he replied and took the phone from his waist and started telling whoever was on the other side exactly what was going on.

"What did you do, Nan?" I asked as my heart slammed against my chest painfully. My throat was tight and I couldn't get a deep breath. I hadn't believed her. I had thought she was trying to get attention. I'd become like everyone else in her life. I had ignored her. I was a horrible brother. I held her against my chest as my phone vibrated in my pocket. I pulled it out and saw Harlow's name on the screen and tossed it aside. I wasn't in the mood to talk to Harlow. She was part of what tormented Nan. I didn't have anything to say to her at the moment.

I rocked Nan in my arms gently. This was Kiro's fault. He'd pay for this. If something happened to her he'd pay for this. "I have you, Nan. I won't leave you but you can't leave me," I whispered as we waited for help.

It felt like forever before I heard feet pounding down the hall and the doorman say, "In here."

Three paramedics came rushing into the room and I handed Nan over to them. They began checking her vitals as I stood there helpless and watched. I heard my phone ring from where I'd tossed it on the floor. I should get it.

"She's taken something. Do you know what it is?" One of the men asked me.

"No, I just got here," I replied numb. She'd overdosed. Holy shit. I ran to the bathroom and found two empty prescription bottles in the sink. Too many painkillers. "FUCK!" I roared. A paramedic was beside me taking the bottles from me.

"We need to get her stomach pumped. Are you family?" He asked.

"Brother," I managed to get out.

"You'll do. Let's get her out of here. You can ride in the ambulance," he replied.

I watched in a daze of disbelief as they put Nan's unresponsive body on a stretcher and began carrying her out of the room. I followed. My phone rang in the distance but I left it. Right now I had to save my sister.

* * *

Six hours later I sat beside Nan's hospital bed. She hadn't woken up yet but the doctor's said they thought she'd have a full recovery. Apparently, I'd found her in time. She'd just passed out from the pills when I'd arrived.

I didn't have my phone and I needed to call Blaire. She'd be worried about me by now. I hadn't been ready to talk to her just yet. This wasn't Blaire's fault but I had been too sensitive to talk to anyone. I had needed them to tell me Nan would live before I could think about anyone or anything else. Now, I felt guilty for not calling Blaire.

Leaving my phone in Nan's hotel hadn't been smart. I had just been in a state of shock and nothing made sense at the time. I was going to get Nan some help and then I was getting Blaire out of LA and back to Rosemary. I needed to call my mother. She should be dealing with this. Not me.

Kiro wasn't going to do anything about it. Nan was wanting something she would never have. It was time she let it go. A nurse opened the door and walked in. I looked up at her and decided it was time I gave up trying to be everything to Nan because I sucked at it.

"I need to speak with the doctor. When she is ready I want her admitted into a facility that will help her get a grip on things. She needs help I can't give her," I said aloud for the first time in my life. I was admitting I'd failed my little sister. Instead of feeling guilty I felt a huge burden lift from my shoulders.

"Doctor Jones will be in shortly. He'll want to admit her as well. She does need help, I'm glad you're in agreement. That always makes these things easier."

Nothing about this would be easy but it was what was best for everyone.

BLAIRE

Rush still wasn't back. He hadn't answered my calls or texts. I'd been at the doctor for over four hours and he hadn't once checked in with me. My baby was okay but the doctor said that I needed to rest, drink more fluids and eliminate stress. The next step would be bed rest if I didn't comply with this. Staying here and dealing with Nan wasn't going to help me. I had to leave.

I glanced at my phone to make sure I hadn't missed a call since the last time I checked it three minutes ago. I was trying not to worry about Rush. I needed to decrease my stress. My baby needed me to.

Harlow had been so quiet in the car. I knew she didn't know what to say. Rush had never shown up or called. She'd tried to call him too. Her silence had been what I needed. I didn't want to talk about it.

Going back to Rosemary didn't sound appealing. Right now I wanted distance from Rush, too. Rosemary would just make me miss him and think about him. A knock on my door broke into my thoughts and I opened it. Dean was standing on the other side looking tired.

"Rush called Kiro and he let him know that he's called Georgianna to come here. We should be expecting her soon. Not sure how long it will take her to get here or where she was to begin with. I just thought you might want a heads up that the wicked queen was on her way here."

Rush had called Kiro was all that I heard. The rest didn't matter. "When did Rush call him?" I asked.

"An hour or so ago, I guess. He just told me."

Rush was fine. He had his phone. He was just choosing not to respond to me. Once again I was faced with the brutal truth that Nan was more important. I nodded and closed the door.

I scrolled my list of contacts until I found my dad's number. He answered on the second ring.

"Blaire?" his surprised voice only reminded me of how little I called him. I could hear the wind from his boat.

"Daddy. I need to get away. Can I come visit?" I asked, refusing to cry. I had made a call like this once before and although he had let me down, in the end I'd thought I had found real happiness. I wasn't so sure anymore.

"Of course. What's wrong?"

"I just can't take it anymore. I need somewhere to think."

"You come to the Key West airport and I'll be there waiting on you. Just let me know when your plane will land."

"Okay, I'll call you with the info as soon as I know. Thank you."

"Don't thank me. I'm your Dad. It's what I'm here for."

I squeezed my eyes tightly closed and hung up the phone. I was really going to leave Rush. My heart was breaking at the thought. I went to my Delta app on my phone and found the first flight out of LAX headed to Atlanta. I'd have a layover there before I got on a plane for Key West. After booking my flight I packed my clothes quickly and called for a cab.

I knew that the grownup thing to do would be to leave Rush a note but I was too mad at him right now. I'd text him later. Maybe after he decided that returning my phone call was important.

No one saw me as I left the house and climbed into the cab. I was thankful. I didn't want to explain myself. I shouldn't have to.

RUSH

Georgianna was headed to LA. She was going with Nan to admit her to the facility that the doctor suggested for her. Our mother would probably make sure it was the best once she got here. I had made sure it was. Georgianna would be more concerned with appearance than Nan's mental well-being. Something was off with Nan and she needed someone to help her. I had a family to take care of. I couldn't keep being responsible for my sister.

Once Nan had woken up and talked to me some I had told her that Mother was on her way. When she'd fallen back to sleep I had left and gone to get my phone. Blaire had called me several times along with Harlow. I had worried her and I had a lot of making up to do. I clicked on the first text from Blaire.

Harlow brought me to her doctor. I was having cramps. They've given me an ultrasound and I'm in a room being monitored.

My stomach dropped. The baby. Oh God, no. I started running for the elevators as I pulled up her next text.

Where are you?

NO! I needed to know if she was okay.

Are you okay?

Fuck! Was she okay? That was it. No more texts from her. I clicked on the first one from Harlow.

Blaire is cramping and bleeding. I brought her to my doctor and they are keeping her here a few hours to observe her and make sure she is okay. Call me, I'll tell you where we are.

That was eight hours ago. FUCK! It was also the only text from Harlow. It was why she'd been trying to call me. NO MORE! NO FUCKING MORE! I was taking Blaire home tonight.

The last text I received from Blaire was five hours ago. Where was she? I dialed her number and it went straight to voicemail. Was she in the hospital? No, no, she couldn't be in the hospital. She had to be okay. Our baby had to be okay. I dialed Harlow's number.

"Hello."

"It's Rush, how's Blaire? Where's Blaire? I didn't have my phone. God, tell me she's okay, please," I rambled into the phone as I ran out the door of the hotel and to my car that I'd had the valet bring up when the taxi had brought me back from the hospital.

"She's okay. I think she's worried about you and maybe . . . hurt," Harlow replied.

A lump formed in my throat and it was hard to swallow. "I'm on my way. Please tell her I'm on my way. Nan took a shitload of painkillers and I've been at that hospital with her. They had to pump her stomach," I explained. I didn't want Blaire mad at me but more importantly I didn't want her hurting.

" Oh. I'm sorry," Harlow simply replied.

"Please tell Blaire. I'm on my way there now," I repeated.

"She didn't come down to dinner and I knocked on her door to take a plate but she didn't answer. I don't want to go in there in case she's sleeping. She's had a long day."

She wasn't eating. She wasn't answering her door. The fear of something happening to her, of finding her like I found Nan terrified me.

"Please go open the door and check on her. Make sure she's okay," I begged.

"Okay," Harlow replied after a pause.

I hung up and threw the phone on the other seat as I sped down Sunset Drive.

When I opened the front door of the house and found Harlow standing in the foyer with my dad, I froze. "What?" I asked, afraid to move.

"She's gone. Her bags are gone. She's not in another room, I checked," Harlow replied.

I shook my head and walked inside. "Gone? She can't be gone? Where would she go?"

"Probably somewhere so she doesn't have to deal with Nan's shit and her fiancé running off and leaving her and not answering her damn calls. That'd be my guess. You're a stupid fucker just like me, son," Dean said with disgust in his voice before walking away.

"I had to tell him why I was running around from room to room checking inside. He caught me," Harlow whispered.

"Did she leave a note?" I asked dialing her number again only to get her voicemail.

Harlow shook her head.

I stalked past her and took the stairs two at a time before breaking into a run yet again. This day had gone from bad to fucking disastrous. Jerking open the bedroom door the silence that met me was knee buckling. I could see the small imprint on the bed from where she'd laid down earlier today. Harlow was right. She was gone. Every little trace of Blaire was gone. She'd needed me. Our baby had needed me and I'd been with Nan, again. I deserve to be left.

I closed the door behind me before leaning against the wall and sliding down to the floor to weep. The fear of losing Nan had been terrifying but the idea of losing Blaire and my baby was unbearable. I didn't deserve Blaire. I had promised her I'd always be there yet my family kept pulling me away.

It was time I stopped letting that happen, but what if I was too late?

I shook my head and wiped the tears from my face. I'd find her and I'd beg. I'd grovel. Whatever I needed to do, I would do it. Then I'd never leave her again. For anyone.

BLAIRE

"Here it is. Ain't much but it's mine," my dad said as he stepped onto a boat with a small cabin that I was sure only had one bed. I was hoping there was a sofa of some kind in there too.

I had been so relieved when I'd stepped off the plane at the small airport to find Abe already there waiting on me. I had worried that I'd spent the last of my savings on airplane tickets to see a man who wouldn't show up. This time he had come through for me.

"Good news is, it's got two bunks and a full size bed. I'll take a bunk and you can have the bed. It'll be easier on you and the baby. I went and got a few things for you at the store. Some things I knew you liked. The fridge is a tiny thing but I have a cooler on here too with ice that I keep cold stuff in."

I stood on the well-worn boat and saw touches of my father. His favorite fishing hat, the one my mother had given him for

Father's Day when I was a little girl, hung on the hook going into the cabin. The tackle box that Valerie and I had saved money one year and bought him for Christmas sat over in the corner with the fishing rod he'd bought one summer when we had gone on a family vacation to a lake house up in North Carolina. I hadn't realized he still had those things.

"It's perfect, Dad. Thanks for letting me come here. I just needed to get away," I said turning to look at him.

His mustache needed trimming as well as his beard but I could still see his mouth turn down in a frown. "What's wrong, Blaire bear? You seemed so happy a week ago. How did things get so bad so fast?"

I didn't want to talk about it just yet. "I slept on the plane and it wasn't good sleep. It's been well over twenty-four hours since I've been in a bed. Can I take a nap first?" I asked.

Dad looked even more upset about my being tired. "You shouldn't have been pushing yourself like that. Why'd you fly overnight? Never mind, you can tell me later. Just go on inside there and head down those steps to that back room. I'll bring your bag down. Not much room but we can manage."

I didn't care about attempting to take a bath in the tiny little bathroom or changing my clothes. I was too tired to care about anything. "I just want some sleep," I assured him.

The bed filled up the entire "bedroom". It touched every wall. I crawled up in it from the doorway and kicked both of my shoes off before curling up into a ball and falling fast asleep.

* * *

It was late afternoon when I woke up. The gentle swaying of the boat was soothing. I was thankful I didn't deal with motion sickness. This would be bad if I did. Stretching I sat up and reached in my pocket to pull out my phone and turn it on. I'd been avoiding this. Rush would know I was gone by now and he would be upset. I wasn't ready to deal with him just yet. I still needed some time to decide what to do.

I didn't check my voicemails or text messages once I turned my phone on. I just slipped it back into my pocket and climbed the steps out of the small cubby hole onto the main deck. Dad wasn't around but he'd mentioned at the airport that he had a job working at the marina and he needed to go in this afternoon. In return they allowed him to keep his boat docked here for free.

The small fridge held a few bottles of water and I took one out and grabbed a banana from the basket of fruit he had sitting on top of the fridge before walking out to sit in the sunshine. It was breezy but sunny. Similar to the temperature in LA.

"Abe know you're on his boat? He don't strike me as the kind to hook up with barely legal women." A deep voice asked from behind me. I spun around to see a guy in his mid twenties standing in the boat docked beside my dad's. He was shirtless and his jeans hung low on his hips. It was obvious he did manual labor. He was slender but solid. His long brown hair was bleached from the sun and it was in a low ponytail. Several strands were loose. I couldn't see his eyes because he was wearing aviators.

"Do you speak?" he asked with a smirk and took a drink from the water bottle in his hand.

"Yes," I replied still slightly startled. I hadn't been expecting Dad to have neighbors. This was a boat for goodness sake. How many people lived on their boats?

"Where's Abe? Or are you crashing?" He was relentless in his questioning.

"I don't know. I just woke up and he was gone," I replied.

The guy raised one of his eyebrows. "So he does know you're here?"

What was he, the damn police? "Abe is my father. He's very aware that I'm here," I replied a little more annoyed than I'd meant to.

A grin broke across his face and he had perfect white teeth. Not what I'd expect from a guy who had hair like his and lived on a boat. "You're Blaire. Nice to meet you. I'm Captain." He replied and took another swig from his water bottle.

"Captain?" I asked before I could stop myself. I knew it sounded rude.

"Yeah," he replied.

"That's just . . . it's an odd name," I replied.

He let out a low chuckle. "Not really. I've been living on this boat since I was sixteen. That's ten years now. Reckon if anyone's a captain I am," he shot me a wink then turned and walked back inside of his cabin.

Left alone again I leaned back in my seat and propped my legs up in front of me on an upside down ten gallon bucket. My phone began ringing and I debated even looking at it. If it was Rush I was going to want to answer it. Maybe it was time I did. He needed to know where to find me.

I glanced down and sure enough Rush's name was on my phone screen. I clicked answer and held it to my ear. I wasn't sure what to say to him. I'd been an emotional mess when I ran. I needed space and time. Now I was missing him. How could I marry him if I couldn't even stand by him when he needed me? Was I always going to get this upset when he wasn't around when I needed him?

"Blaire? Please, God, tell me you answered this phone," Rush's voice was laced with panic. I felt guilty.

"It's me," I replied.

"Where are you, baby? Please tell me where you are. I swear I won't ever leave you again. I'm done with dealing with my sister's shit and being the parent my parents weren't. I just need you. Please, where are you? I'm in Rosemary and you're not here." He was so worried. I'd scared him. My throat tightened and my eyes stung.

"I'm in Key West with my dad," I replied.

"Fuck. Did he come get you from the airport? Are you staying on his boat? Did he feed you?" Rush paused in his many questions and took a deep breath. I could tell he was trying to calm himself down.

"He did come get me and I'm fine. He had bought some groceries before I got here so I've eaten," I paused and squeezed my eyes tightly shut in order to hold back my tears. I didn't want to cry. Rush would completely go insane if he heard me crying. "I'm sorry. I was upset and I needed to get away from it all. I needed time to think."

"I know you're upset. You had every fucking right to be upset. You went through a scare without me and I hate myself for it. You should have left me. Hell, I would have left me," he stopped and took a deep breath. "Can I come get you? Please? I need you, Blaire."

Would it always be like this? Would I always come second to Nan? Would our baby come second? I knew he believed he was done with her but I knew better. He loved his sister and when she needed him it would kill him to ignore her. I guess what I needed to ask myself was *could I live without him?*

No. It was that simple. Even with my heart still hurting from him not being there for me and the baby when I needed him, I still couldn't imagine life without him.

"Nan had overdosed. I found her unconscious in her hotel room. I left my phone in her room when I rushed off with the paramedics to take her to the hospital. That's why I didn't answer you. I'm so sorry, Blaire. I am so damn sorry," the pleading in his voice broke my heart. I should have known it was something that serious. Rush always answered my calls and text.

"Is Nan okay?" I asked. Not because I cared about Nan but because I cared about Rush.

"Yeah. They pumped her stomach. My mother is taking her to a center in Montana to get her some help. I can't keep trying to control her. I have you and our baby to focus on."

I looked up as my dad stepped into the boat. He was carrying a paper bag in one hand and a gallon of sweet tea in the other. I wasn't ready to leave him just yet. I had just got here and I liked seeing him happy. Or at least, content.

"I want to stay and visit my dad for a little while," I told him knowing he was going to argue. I was missing him something fierce and I knew he felt the same way.

"Okay. Can I come visit him too?" he asked

My dad was watching me, and a small smile tugged on his lips. I didn't have to tell him what Rush had asked. He already knew. "Tell the boy to come on. I got room for one more."

"I'd like that. I miss you," I replied.

Rush let out a sigh. "God, baby, I miss you too. So damn much. I'll be there as soon as I can get a flight out."

RUSH

I needed to get to Blaire. I needed to hold her and reassure myself I hadn't just lost her, and that she and our baby were okay. Then I was convincing her to go home with me and marry me immediately. I didn't want to wait anymore. I shouldn't have waited this long.

My plane had landed thirty minutes ahead of schedule. We'd taken off earlier than planned. I didn't want to wait around until the time I'd told her to be here and I didn't want her coming to the airport alone. I grabbed a cab and told them to take me to the marina. I'd find Abe's boat myself. Key West wasn't a big place. I'd find her before she had time to leave.

Stepping onto the pier that went between the rows of docked boats I looked for any sign of Blaire or Abe. I'd called her but it had gone straight to voicemail. There were sailboats, fishing boats and even houseboats docked in this place. Several of them had people living on board. I was getting close to the end when I saw a guy standing near the back of his boat. He had his arms crossed over his bare chest as he stared over at the boat next to him. I started to ask him if he knew where Abe Wynn's boat was when I followed his gaze.

Long blonde hair hung down her back and blew carelessly in the wind. The short familiar sundress she was wearing was a favorite of hers lately because it was one of the few things that still fit her. The small stomach that had developed over the past weeks was taking up more room and the length on it was shorter than I preferred. Taking in the sight of her I felt whole again . . . until I realized that she was what the shirtless guy was staring at. She didn't realize it because her back was turned and she was looking out at the clear blue water as the sun set sending off an array of colors. But I saw it.

My inner caveman wanted to go jerk him off his boat and throw his ass in the water. I couldn't do that though. As pissed off as it made me to know he was looking at what was mine, I understood why. She was breathtaking. I wanted to stop and stare at her too.

I took the other caveman route and headed straight for her father's boat and jumped on then pulled her into my arms before she could spin around to see who it was.

"Rush," she said in a contented sigh and the caveman felt like pounding on his chest. She knew it was me. I loved that. I buried my nose in the crook of her neck and inhaled deeply. She smelled so damn good. Today her sweet smell was mixed with the sea. I wanted to strip her naked and find out if she smelled like the sea everywhere else too.

I placed both my hands over her stomach just to remind myself that our baby was still okay. He was healthy and Blaire was fine. Every time I thought about her bleeding and cramping my heart felt as if it had stopped. I'd basically abandoned her the last few days trying to get Nan under control so I could leave. My last words to Blaire had been harsh and that was all I could think about when I'd found her gone. Had my words made her cramp? I didn't deserve her but I wasn't going to let her go. "I'm sorry. God, Blaire, I am so damn sorry. I love you. This will never happen again," I promised even though the words sounded familiar to my ears. I winced, realizing I'd said this before. I should have never gone to LA.

"I love you," she replied simply.

"I love you too," I replied holding her as we stood there watching the sunset over the water.

When the dusk was finally settling down around us I bent my head down to her ear. "Is there a hotel we could sleep in tonight? I'm gonna need you and it won't be quiet."

Blaire turned around in my arms and slipped her arms around my waist. Her green eyes were twinkling with amusement. "I can be quiet," she replied.

I reached up and tucked a strand of her hair behind her ear. Then traced her jawline before feeling her soft plump bottom lip. "I can't."

A pleased smile pulled up each corner of her mouth and she stood on her tiptoes to press a kiss to my mouth. "You can whisper your naughty words in my ear," she replied.

I pulled her bottom lip into my mouth and sucked on it before slipping my tongue inside her mouth to taste her. She clung to my arms and moaned softly and swayed into me. Fuck no was I gonna be quiet tonight. "Unless you want your daddy hearing me groan from the sweet taste of your pussy and cry out your name when I come inside of you, then we need a fucking hotel."

Blaire pressed her body closer to mine and a soft moan escaped her. "God, Rush. I swear if you keep talking like that I'm gonna have an orgasm right here."

I cupped her ass and pulled her up against me before covering her mouth with mine again. If she was that swollen and turned on that words could get her off then I was going to fucking make that happen.

A loud cough caused Blaire to freeze in my arms then she slowly eased back from me and peeked over my shoulder. Her cheeks turned bright pink and she ducked her head into my chest. The fact she was burying herself against me was the only thing that kept me from losing it. I didn't like the idea that him seeing us together embarrassed her.

I glanced back over my shoulder to see the guy I'd seen watching her when I walked up. Having Blaire in my arms again made me forget all about everything around us. Not that it would have mattered. I wanted him to know she was mine. I wanted everyone to know.

"Thought y'all might wanna get a room," the guy said with a smirk and lit a cigarette.

"We're just fine. Maybe you need to find another direction to look in," I replied. I made sure the warning was in my voice.

The guy chuckled and blew a puff of smoke. "Watching the sun set is my thing. Shame if a guy can't watch something that beautiful from his own boat."

The flicker in his eyes as he glanced down at Blaire in my arms made my blood boil. Blaire must have felt me tense up because she instantly flattened herself against me and pressed a kiss to my chest. "Let's go inside. I want some alone time with you," she said just loud enough for me to hear.

I looked back down at her and relaxed. She was mine. I needed to calm the fuck down. "Lead the way."

Blaire grabbed both my arms and pulled me into the small kitchen. I could see the door that led down into the boat and the idea of getting tucked away down there with Blaire was pretty damn appealing. "How much longer until your dad gets home?" I asked walking her back towards the stairs.

"Not sure," she replied with a giggle.

"Does that bedroom have a door with a lock?"

BLAIRE

"Yes, but I'm not sure when Daddy will be home. We can't just go in there," I replied unable to keep from laughing at him.

"Sweet Blaire, if I don't get inside you real damn fast more than just your daddy is gonna know we're having sex. That little kitchen table is looking real nice right about now."

I shivered with anticipation as he pulled me down into the lower room.

"Just a bed," he said, as he looked at the small room. "Hell, yeah."

I crawled up on the unmade bed and he followed me before turning to close the sliding pocket door and locking it. His dirty talk and my horny state had me so worked up that it wasn't going to take much to send me off. I was trembling with the need for him to touch me.

"Take it off," he said, looking pointedly down at my sundress.

I reached for the hem and pulled it over my head before tossing it to the side of the mattress. I hadn't bothered with a bra but I was wearing panties. His eyes flared with heat as he gazed at my breasts. I loved knowing that the sight of my swollen stomach didn't make him want me any less. If anything he was even more attracted to me.

He pulled his shirt off then crawled over to kneel in front of me. His large hands cupped my breasts and he teased my nipples causing me to moan and press myself further into his hands. He let his hands move south until he was covering my stomach with both of his hands and gently caressing me. "Mine," he said simply, with wonder and awe in his voice.

Then his hand slipped down between my legs and into the panties I was still wearing. He found out just exactly how turned on I was. "Mmmm, my sweet Blaire needs me. I like that. I fucking love it," he groaned and laid me back on the mattress before pulling my panties off. He ran his thumb over the pads of my feet then wrapped a hand around each of my ankles and pulled them over his shoulders.

"Rush," I tried to stop him before he started just because I wanted him inside me. But his tongue flicked out over my folds and licked all the way up to my clit causing all reasonable thought to fly away. I grabbed handfuls of the sheets and bucked against his face as I cried out his name. I no longer cared who heard me. The smooth metal in his mouth teased my clit relentlessly as he ran it back and forth over my swollen sex.

"So damn sweet," he murmured against me and I fell apart. My body convulsed and I was sure I screamed his name loud enough for our neighbors to hear. When I managed to get my eyes open again, he was naked and moving up between my legs.

I lifted to meet his thrust and loved watching his face contort with pleasure as he whispered my name this time.

Rush reached down and pulled my hips up to meet his thrusts as he slid in and out of me in a steady rhythm. I felt the pleasure building again and I became more frantic to feel it again. I began lifting my hips higher as I grabbed his arms to pull myself up faster.

Rush stopped and eased me back slowing the pace as he moved over me. His mouth covered mine and he began kissing me as if he had all the time in the world, when in reality, I was a few thrusts away from another orgasm. His tongue ran across mine tangling with it and then licking at my lips before pressing chaste kisses on the corners of my mouth and then sucking on my top lip. "Don't leave me again. I can't lose you," he pleaded.

His hips moved and pressed into me deep one more time as he let out a groan. I went flying apart clinging to him and promising him anything he wanted. His cry of release sent me off again.

When I finally managed to breathe, Rush was cuddling me into his arms and tucking his head into the crook of my neck. His warm breath tickled and soothed me at the same time.

"Love you. So fucking much," he said in a husky whisper.

"I love you too. So fucking much," I replied with a happy smile.

He chuckled but didn't look at me. He kept his face buried against me. "I'm gonna need you again. I'm sorry," he said.

Confused, I frowned and pulled back so I could see his face. "Why are you sorry?"

"Because I may be insatiable tonight. It's been a long twenty-four hours."

"You mean you want more, now?" I asked

Rush slipped his hands between my legs. "Yeah, baby, I do."

Rush was asleep when I heard my dad enter the boat. I was thankful he'd missed out on all the action. Rush had finally fallen asleep from exhaustion. I was completely satisfied though. I'd fought off sleep because I wanted to wait for my dad to come back home. I reached for my sundress and eased out of Rush's arms then slipped it over my head. I needed to go tell him about Rush being here. I hadn't told him much of anything so he needed some explaining.

Unlocking the door, I glanced back at Rush who was still sleeping peacefully. Easing off the bed and out of the room I tiptoed up stairs. Dad was sitting at the kitchen table fixing himself a glass of milk. He glanced over at me and smiled. "Didn't mean to wake you," he said.

"You didn't. I was awake," I replied. I nodded towards the front of the boat, outside where our voice wouldn't carry downstairs as loudly. "Can we talk?"

Dad looked towards the stairs and frowned then nodded and stood up to walk back outside of the cabin.

I closed the cabin door to muffle anything we said before turning to look at my dad. "Rush is here," I explained. "He's sleeping."

Understanding dawned on my dad's face and he nodded. "Good. Glad the boy was smart enough to come get you."

He liked Rush. He'd thrown me in front of Rush to begin with. I was glad he approved of Rush. That made things so much easier. I wanted to keep a relationship with my dad and Rush hadn't been a fan of him for a long time.

"I left because of his family. Nan mostly. She's . . . too much sometimes."

"She's a nightmare. She isn't my daughter so you can be blunt. I spent enough time with her to know she's in need of some serious attention from a father."

I nodded and sat down on the bench seat along the side of the boat then tucked my legs underneath me. "I don't want to hate her because Rush loves her. It's hard though. She's determined to take him away from me. Sometimes I think she just might win."

Dad sat down on a faded rainbow colored lawn chair. "Boy loves you more. He will always love you more. Anyone can see that, baby girl. You just have to learn not to let Nan intimidate you."

"I'm trying. But then when she needs him, he is there. Most of the time at the expense of when I need him. She always wins.

I know that sounds silly and I'm being selfish, but I need him to pick me. I need him to pick me and our baby over everyone else. I don't . . . I don't know if he'll ever do that," saying the words aloud caused my throat to constrict. Admitting your worst fear was hard. But I needed someone to listen to me.

"You deserve to be number one. You've been through too much shit thanks to me, and it's time a man made you feel like you're the most important person in his world. It isn't selfish. It's normal. That sister of his uses the fact she was deprived of a father as her excuse to be a raging spoiled bitch. You were handed an even shittier deal. You lost your sister. Your father, and your mother. You've had more pain than that girl could ever understand yet you still love. You still forgive and you're strong. You'll be an incredible mother and wife." Dad let out a heavy sigh. "All Rush's life he's thought of Nan as his child. He's raised her. She's an adult now and it's time he let go. He's figuring out how to do that and I think he'll find it. He loves you. I know he does. Any fool can see it all over his face."

I hoped he was right. "I love him enough that I'm afraid even if he always chooses her, I will always forgive him."

Dad nodded and leaned forward to rest his elbows on his knees. "I reckon if that happens then I'll have to fly back to Alabama to beat the shit outta the boy. You just call me. I'll always come get you."

I smiled at the sincere look on his face as he threatened to beat up Rush for me. This was the man I'd grown up loving. This was the man who threatened Cain with his hunting rifle on our first date. I stood up and walked over to him and wrapped my arms around his neck. "I love you," I whispered.

"Love you too, Blaire bear."

A loud cough startled me and I glanced back to see the guy from earlier, once again standing on his boat watching us. He was beginning to give me the creeps. At least this time he was wearing a shirt, even if it was unbuttoned and hanging open.

"Evening, Captain" Dad called out and the guy raised his beer in a greeting.

"Evening," he replied. But he didn't leave. He just stood there.

"This is Blaire. My daughter," he replied.

"We met earlier today," he told Abe and winked at me again. I immediately felt uncomfortable. Rush wouldn't like him winking at me. Maybe we shouldn't stay a few days. I was pregnant. Couldn't he see that? Why would he be flirting with a pregnant woman?

"Ah, well then, good. Glad y'all met," Dad sounded nervous. Something was off. Was this guy dangerous?

The door to the cabin opened and a sleep ruffled Rush walked outside. This time he was shirtless and his jeans were unbuttoned. I doubted he'd even put on his underwear. He looked like he'd just woken up, realized I was missing and jerked on his jeans to come and find me. His eyes shifted from me to Captain and back. The angry snarl on his face surprised me. He hadn't seen the man wink at me had he?

"Hello, Abe," he said in a sleepy voice as he walked over and pulled me against him. Yes, he was definitely asserting his possession. Why would he feel threatened? Did the man not understand that I was completely obsessed with him?

"Rush. Even though I was real happy to see Blaire, I'm glad you were smart enough to come get her," Abe replied. The warning in his tone was unmistakable. He was letting Rush know he didn't like me feeling second.

Rush nodded and pressed his lips to my head. "It won't happen again," he told my father.

Dad nodded. "Good. Next time I won't be so understanding," he told him.

"Newlyweds?" Captain asked, still standing there watching us.

Rush tensed and I eased closer to him to calm him down. He wanted to be a newlywed. Having another guy question our relationship bothered him.

"They're engaged," Dad explained.

Captain pointed the beer towards me as if he was pointing at my stomach. "Got things a little backwards don't you," the accusation in his voice caused Rush to move before I could stop him. He was around me and moving across the boat immediately. I reached out and grabbed Rush's arm just as his foot hit the step leading out.

"Alright, hold it," Dad said in a loud commanding voice I wasn't used to hearing. "I was gonna wait and explain this to Blaire without a damn audience, but it looks like I need to do it now. Since you've done gone and pissed Rush off." He was shooting Captain an annoyed look.

What was he talking about? What kind of explanation?

Rush stopped moving and glared back at my father. "No one talks to Blaire like that. I don't give a fuck who he is."

"Wasn't talking to Blaire. I was talking to you," Captain drawled in a bored tone and took another swig of his beer.

I wrapped both hands around Rush's arm and held on tight.

"That's enough, boy," Dad snapped at Captain. I would like to argue that he wasn't a boy but a man who could very likely hurt my dad without breaking a sweat. I preferred that he stayed friendly with his neighbors.

Captain held up both his hands and shrugged. "Fine," he replied. I was shocked that he backed down so easily.

Dad sighed and looked back at me. "You might want to sit back down," he said.

I wasn't sure I wanted to hear this. Why would I need to sit down? Rush instantly moved and took my seat then pulled me into his lap and wrapped his arms around my waist.

Dad looked over at Captain and frowned. He didn't want to tell me whatever it was that he was about to tell me. That made me nervous.

"When I was sixteen I knocked up my high school girlfriend," he started and I grabbed Rush's arms and held on tight. "Becca Lynn wasn't ready to be a momma and I sure as hell wasn't ready to be a daddy. We agreed to put the baby up for adoption. Becca Lynn's parents handled the finding of suitable parents for the baby and then she had it and that was it. We didn't stay together. We'd broken up with the reality of her pregnancy and what had happened. After graduation she went on to college on the west coast and I went to Georgia. Never saw her again," my dad said and sighed. He studied me a moment before going any further. Rush's arms had tightened around me and I was holding onto him. I wasn't sure yet where exactly this was going but I had an idea.

"After you and Valerie were born, I realized how precious you were and I loved you both so damn much, I broke down one night and told your mother about the baby I'd had with Becca Lynn and given up eight years before. For the first time I was broken up about losing a kid I had thought I didn't want. Your mother made it her goal to find my child. She looked for years. Everything always led to another dead end. I eventually gave up. She never did," Dad let out a sad laugh. "Then last year I was contacted by the investigator your mother had hired and he had a lead. I hadn't been expecting it. I didn't know what to do with that information now. That kid was now an adult. I was sure it was pointless. Then I got another call. My son wanted to meet me."

I turned in Rush's arms to look at Captain. He was leaning against his boat looking out over the water but he was listening. His body was tense. He was waiting. Was he . . . did I have a brother?

"Everything happened with you and I came clean. I needed to start over. Try to live the rest of my life the right way because all I'd done was fuck it up so far. The only good thing I'd ever done was love your mother and be blessed with you and Valerie. So, I called my son and came down south to meet him," he paused and nodded to Captain. "River Joshua Kipling, also known as Captain, is your brother."

"Fuck," Rush whispered and I felt like saying it too. Would my dad's secrets never end?

"Captain was your mother's last gift to me. If she hadn't been so determined to find him then I never would have gotten to know him."

My dad wasn't as alone as I'd thought. I wasn't angry or hurt. I was . . . happy. I was relieved. He had a lot in life to atone for and I knew he was trying to make up for not being the man he should've been for so long by having a relationship with his son.

My baby kicked against his father's hands and I couldn't imagine handing over this baby. To never know it, or hold it. That had to be like losing a part of yourself. My dad hadn't been a whole man since he was sixteen. Since he'd given a part of himself away. My heart broke for him and I eased out of Rush's arms and walked over to my father.

I wrapped both arms around his waist and held him. I didn't have the words just yet to tell him that I was happy for him. I wasn't sure if those words were even accurate. I was more than happy. I was thankful. It was time for him to heal. This was a part of that.

"You okay with this, Blaire bear?" he asked, squeezing me in a hug.

"I'm glad you found him," I replied honestly. For right now that was the only thing I could say.

"Thank you," the emotion in his voice was thick.

"Real glad I don't have to beat your ass for looking at my woman," I heard Rush say and I smiled against my dad's chest.

RUSH

We stayed for five more days to let Blaire get to know her brother. Captain was a lot easier to tolerate once I realized he wasn't checking Blaire out in a sexual way. He was just curious about his sister. I understood that. But I was also glad to pack up and go home. It was only three weeks until Christmas and I wanted to spend that in Rosemary with Blaire. In our home. I also wanted to pin my last name on her and beat on my chest like a fucking crazy man.

Blaire had gone straight to bed when we got back to Rosemary. She smiled happily when we walked inside then looked at me and told me unless I just wanted to snuggle to leave her alone while she went to take a nap.

I was pretty sure I wouldn't be able to just snuggle so I stayed downstairs and enjoyed being home. I got a soda from the fridge and headed out to sit on the deck and enjoy the gulf. I'd missed it. I hadn't even gotten comfortable when I heard the door behind me open.

Grant walked out and nodded at me before taking the seat beside me. We hadn't spoken since the day before Thanksgiving when I'd called him about Nan. I had been busy and I was sure he was dodging me. Apparently, the Rosemary radar was out because we hadn't been back in town for thirty minutes and he was already at my house. I hadn't even realized Grant was in town. Normally he spent his winters skiing. Last I'd heard he was headed to Vail.

"How is she?" was the first words out of his mouth.

He wasn't asking about Blaire. I knew from the sad tone in his voice that this was about Nan. "Fucked the hell up. You know that."

Grant let out a sigh, stretched his legs out in front of him and crossed them at the ankles. "Yeah I know. But I called her last night because I was drunk and weak and being stupid as shit. Your mother answered. She said Nan was getting help."

"She tried to overdose. I found her and got her to the hospital in time. She was okay physically but mentally she has snapped. Kiro is a shit for a dad and Harlow knows that, but Nan will never accept it the way Harlow has."

"Who's Harlow?" Grant asked and I realized that there were parts of my life that even Grant didn't know. I had kept my life in Rosemary separate from my life with my dad.

"Kiro's other daughter. The one he did take care of, or at least, left her with a grandmother that loved her and kept her far away from his fucked up world. Harlow was his shiny toy he went and got every once and awhile and then sent her back to her grandmother when being a Dad got in his way. It worked for him because Harlow is quiet, polite and stays out of the way. Nan is none of those things. So, he has no use for her."

Grant let out a deep sigh. "Damn."

Damn wasn't even scratching the surface.

We sat in silence for awhile and stared out at the water. I wasn't sure how deep he was in with Nan but I hoped he could walk away. She wasn't stable. She never would be. Not enough to make Grant happy.

"You gonna get married anytime soon?" Grant finally asked.

Smiling, I thought about Blaire curled up in my bed upstairs . . . our bed upstairs. "Yeah. When she wakes up from her nap, I'm letting her know that she has a week to plan it. I can't wait any longer. I've waited long enough."

Grant chuckled. "I'm the best man right?"

"Of course. I'm afraid you'll be stuck with Bethy as a partner though so get ready for Jace to be breathing down your neck like a crazy motherfucker. I have no doubt that Bethy will be her maid of honor. The other option will be Jimmy and I doubt you want him groping your ass."

"I can deal with Bethy and Jace," Grant replied in an amused tone. "But is Jimmy really going to be a bridesmaid?"

I grinned and nodded. "Yep. She asked him when we first started planning this wedding."

I had left plane tickets with both Abe and Captain before we left. Blaire wanted her father here and, after watching her and Captain get to know each other, I knew she'd want her brother here too. They had both agreed to come up for it in a week. Blaire didn't know about it yet though. I hadn't been in the mood to argue with her in case she had a reason to put it off.

"Nan coming to the wedding?" Grant asked.

I never imagined I'd get married without my mom and sister being in attendance. However, I wanted nothing to spoil our wedding memories for Blaire and I knew that they would somehow manage to do just that. I wouldn't allow it.

"No. I can't have her here. She still hates Blaire," I replied.

Grant nodded and his shoulders relaxed. He hadn't wanted to see her. That much was obvious. I couldn't blame him.

"You know dumbass Woods is gonna marry that chick from New York his parents want him to. He isn't engaged yet but he will be soon. He admitted to me over tequila the other night that if he wanted the club then he had to marry her. His dad's forcing his hand. He's gonna be miserable with that uptight woman."

I hated that for Woods. I knew what it felt like to anticipate your wedding and the rest of your life with the woman you loved. Everyone should know that feeling. Going into it with regret and bitterness wasn't the way to get married.

"His choice I guess. He could always say no."

"And run off like Tripp? That ain't a great plan either," Grant replied.

Tripp had been a few years older than us. He was Jace's cousin and we'd all looked up to him. Then his parents pressured him to lead the life they wanted and he bolted. Left his millions behind and fucking ran. He became immortalized in our eyes as teenagers because he had the balls to say fuck off and leave. Now we were older we understood more about the sacrifice he made. I just hoped he was happy.

"Better choice than marrying a spoiled bitch," I said.

"True," Grant paused and reached for my soda to take a drink. The dickhead knew I wouldn't drink after him now. "How's your dad?"

"Same. Drinks and smokes too much. Has sex with random women my age. You know the drill."

Grant smiled. "Yeah. But what a life."

It wasn't a life at all but I knew Grant wouldn't agree with me so I let it go. He hadn't found someone like Blaire so he didn't have a clue just how shallow my dad's life really was. He had to be lonely.

"Everyone knows y'all are back in town. You up for company tonight?"

No. I wanted Blaire all to myself. We'd been sharing a boat with her dad for five days too long. "Not tonight. Blaire needs her rest."

"Or you just need Blaire. Be honest, bro."

"Yeah, I need Blaire." I replied with a smile.

BLAIRE

Rush had set the date for our wedding. He'd given me one week. I didn't even try to argue. The determination in his eyes had told me there was no point. I was more than ready to marry the man but I got the feeling he was worried that I would back out. Especially after what happened at his dad's with Nan.

We would be getting married twelve days before Christmas. The plan was to spend Christmas and New Years at home together, then leave New Years day to go on an extended honeymoon. He had been torn between wanting to take me all over the world and not wanting to make me travel too much. He was worried about keeping me rested. Which was also making wedding preparations difficult. In the end I had convinced him that staying in his penthouse in Manhattan was what I wanted to do. I had never been to New York so it was an adventure for me. We would also have the comfort of his home there and my obstetrician was going to set me up with one there to check on me while I was away.

Luckily Rush had the money to make this wedding happen fast and still be beautiful. I'd wanted things simple and I'd wanted to get married here at our house. Surprisingly, simple took a lot of preparation too. I wouldn't have been able to pull any of it off without Bethy's help. Jimmy had been a lot of help too but he and Bethy had almost killed each other more than once. They were fighting for who was in control.

Rush had hired Henrietta to come stay with us for the entire week before the wedding. Seeing Henrietta go into the pantry each night to go to her room under the stairs to sleep always made me smile. I had fond memories of that room.

When the doorbell rang after breakfast I had jumped up and hurried to get it. I was expecting my dad and Captain today. Tonight was the wedding rehearsal and I needed Dad here to practice walking me down the aisle. Jerking the door open I was surprised to find Dean and Harlow instead. I hadn't expected them until tomorrow.

"Surprise, we're here a day early. I didn't want to miss any festivities," Dean said with a smirk and walked inside the house carrying his bag and letting Harlow carry hers as she walked in quietly behind him. "Where's my boy?" Dean asked, looking around.

"Rush left this morning to pick up tuxes with Grant," I explained. "They'll be back soon. Come on up and I'll show you to your room Harlow. Dean, I assume you know where yours is?"

"Yeah, I'll go up to mine in a few. I need a drink and some sunshine."

I smiled over at Harlow. "I picked out my favorite room for you. It has the best view. Used to be my room," I told her.

"Thank you. I hate to take up one of the best rooms though. I'll gladly take the smallest one. I know you have family coming in too," she said and paused on the top step.

"My dad and my . . . um . . . my brother live on old fishing boats. Trust me when I tell you that the smallest room we have here will be all they desire. I want you to enjoy this room. It's farther away from everyone too. So you'll have more privacy."

Harlow smiled shyly and nodded. I led her back to the room I'd once stayed in maybe twice if that many times. I had kept my things in here for awhile once I'd moved upstairs.

"Was the flight good?" I asked when I really wanted to ask how things were at home.

"It was nice. I watched Pride and Prejudice again. Made the trip go by quicker."

"I love that movie," I admitted. "So, how are things at home? With Nan gone?" Rush hadn't brought up Nan once since we'd been home. I knew she wasn't invited to the wedding and it made me feel so guilty. But the fear that she would make a scene and ruin our wedding was real.

"Quiet again. Dad does his thing. I do mine. Dean does his.

They'll be going on tour in a couple of months and it will be really quiet."

I felt sad for her. She didn't have anyone really. Living in that big house with a father like Kiro had to be lonely. Then with him gone and it just her being there. That was no life at all. Money couldn't buy you everything. Harlow was proof of that.

"Why don't you have Kiro buy you a house here? It's beautiful here and there are people our age everywhere. Cute guys." I flashed her a teasing smile. As perfect as Harlow looked appearance wise I couldn't imagine her with a guy. She was so shy. How would she ever open up to one and get to know him?

"I can't ask Dad that. I'm at UCLA on a full ride scholarship. He would have to pay for my tuition if I went somewhere else. And I do get out and go to my classes," she trailed off. I knew from being there that although she went to her classes she had no friends.

"I think he can afford it," I assured her.

She shrugged but didn't reply. I wasn't going to badger her now. Maybe later. "I need to go get dressed. I have a salon appointment for a manicure and pedicure in an hour. You wanna come?"

She shook her head. "No, thank you. I think I'll just take a nap. We left so early and I didn't sleep any on the plane."

Nodding, I took that as my cue to leave her alone.

* * *

It was late in the afternoon when my dad and Captain arrived. I was just finishing up getting ready for the rehearsal and the party that followed. We were having a wedding party in the ballroom at the Club. I hadn't wanted a bachelorette party and Rush hadn't wanted me to have one either. He'd been worried about where Bethy might take me. Then when Grant had brought up the bachelor party he had quickly shot that idea down. This was our alternative. We decided to party together with all of our friends. Woods had gladly supplied the ballroom for us and had his kitchen staff catering it.

The rehearsal was in thirty minutes and people would start arriving any minute. Rush walked down the stairs in a pair of tan slacks and a white linen shirt and my heart missed more than one beat. He was beautiful. His hair was styled in a messy look now that he'd let it grow out enough so that he could do that and his silver eyes looked brighter and his skin darker in contrast to the white shirt.

"You're gorgeous," I breathed as he came to a stop at the bottom of the steps.

"Hey, that's my line," he teased pulling me to him and pressing a kiss to my lips. "You're breathtaking," he replied.

"Mmmm, so are you," I murmured against his lips.

GRANT

(YES YOU READ THAT CORRECTLY)

My brother was actually getting married. I knew it would happen the first time I saw him go ape shit crazy over Blaire, but damn, actually seeing them rehearse it had been real. Too damn real. I felt like I was losing him a little. It wasn't that I wasn't happy for him because I was. It was just that he'd been my partner in crime for as long as I could remember. Now he would be Blaire's.

I took a glass of champagne from the tray as a server walked by me. I might as well take the bubbly shit until I could get something real at the bar in a few minutes. Scanning the crowd I thought about Nan and how fucked up I'd let shit get. I needed something to help me forget her. Not that I wasn't over her because I was. She'd made sure of it. Crazy bitch.

A pair of the sexiest eyes I'd ever seen locked with mine and I froze and studied her. I hadn't seen her before. Ever. I'd never forget those fucking eyes. It wasn't the color that drew me in because from here I couldn't tell what the color was. It was the slant to them and the heavy eyelashes that fanned over them. Women paid good money for false eyelashes that could never look that good. I trailed my eyes down her face until I landed on one big ass mouth. SHIT. My cock stirred to life. It was wide and her lips were so damn full. A girl with a mouth like that was every man's fantasy.

I was almost afraid to let my gaze travel any further. If it kept getting better I was going to fucking unload in my damn pants. I didn't have time to think about it though because she turned and like a wisp of air, she was gone. Long brown hair swayed as she moved brushing just above of her waist. Holy mother of Jesus, her hair was all the way to her perfect little ass. I took off after her. I didn't know who the hell she was but she wasn't getting away from me. I needed to have a taste of that mouth and see her eyes light up with pleasure as I pulled that long hair back and pounded into her.

Talk about a fucking distraction. She was the only damn distraction any man needed for anything. Hell, she could make me forget my own damn name. She slipped out of the ballroom and into the hall walking quickly but so quietly no one around her seemed to notice. How did people not notice her? Was I hallucinating? What man with a cock didn't lock eyes on her and not drink her every move in?

I stepped into the hall seconds after her and glanced around. At first I thought I'd lost her but then I noticed movement to the right and the long brown hair was peeking around the corner. She didn't see me but I sure as hell saw that hair. I walked as quietly as I could in her direction.

"Calm down. It was just a guy. A really, really hot one, but just a guy," I heard her voice saying softly as I got closer to her. What the fuck?

"Deep breaths. You're a big girl. You can handle a guy looking at you," she said in the same hushed whisper.

I stopped before I got close enough for her to see me. She was talking to herself. I'd made her nervous. How? When a female looked like that she had to be used to guys eye fucking her from across the room. She started chanting that I was just a guy again and I couldn't keep the grin off my face. That was just all kinds of adorable.

"He could be an alien from Krypton. Then you'd need to be worried. Maybe we should go check him out and make sure," I said casually. Her entire body tensed and she didn't move a muscle. Nor did she turn around and look at me. She kept her back pressed against the wall she'd been hiding behind. The only thing that moved was her hand. It looked like she'd used it to cover her mouth. She just kept getting cuter.

"Probably safe. Rush and Blaire don't much care for the alien sort. They're prejudiced that way," I continued, hoping my ridiculous conversation would make her smile and relax. Because I wanted her relaxed. At least enough so that I could get a taste.

She still didn't move. Her hand remained firmly over her mouth and she was frozen in place. I stepped up around the corner and into the small cubbyhole she'd found between two pillars in the wall. Even with my back pressed against the other wall our bodies were almost touching. Her eyes went wide with surprise as I slipped into her hiding spot with her.

"I'm guessing you can't talk much with your hand over your mouth like that. How exactly do you plan on talking to me?" I asked and smiled encouragingly. I didn't want her to think I was dangerous.

She slowly moved her hand away and let it fall to her side but she remained plastered against the other wall as if to get as far away from me as possible.

"That's better. I like looking at that mouth of yours. You were hindering the view," I said, then winked. She flattened herself further against the wall. This had to be the oddest experience I'd ever had with a female. Most of them threw themselves at me and it was easy. I liked it. Less work. But damned if I wasn't enjoying this one and her skittish behavior. It was refreshing and unique.

"I'm Grant. Brother of the groom," I explained, hoping that would calm her a little. It worked. She frowned and a wrinkle between her eyebrows appeared making her perfect face more human. More accessible. I liked it. A lot. Maybe I could make her frown more.

"Rush doesn't have a brother," she replied matter of factly.

So she knew Rush. Interesting. I'd never seen her or I sure as hell would have remembered. I'd assumed she was with a guest or knew Blaire somehow. There were a few people here I didn't know tonight. "Well, that's where you're wrong, beautiful. Rush and I became stepbrothers when we were kids. Just because our parents didn't make it doesn't mean we didn't."

Her eyes flickered with recognition. She knew who I was. Time for fair play. I wanted to know who she was.

"Want to tell me who you are? Since you've obviously figured out who I am."

Her eyes dropped from my gaze to study the floor. "I think I need to go back inside," she whispered. Her already soft voice was even softer when she whispered. I wondered if she was so quiet and mannerly when she was coming. At the moment that was all I could think about. All I wanted to know.

"You can't leave me now. If you go back in there I'm going to stalk you all night," I warned, hoping it didn't make me sound like a psycho.

That mouth of hers made an "O" shape and my imagination went wild. I wasn't one to be attracted to the uptight female but this prim and proper attitude coming from a walking sexual fantasy was working for me.

"Why?" she asked. The musical sound of her voice reminded me of tinkling bells often overlooked in songs because of their simple beauty.

"You want the truth?" I asked, leaning closer to her and invading the personal space she was trying so hard to protect.

"Please," she replied so softly I almost didn't hear her.

"Because all I can think about is the way those eyes of yours would look flashing with need and the way your fucking amazing mouth would look as you cry out from pleasure. And this hair," I replied, slipped my hands into it and tugging gently. "Fuck me, baby, this hair should be illegal." I'd gotten too close and her breathing was short and quick. And damn it all to hell she smelled amazing. Like strawberries and cream.

"Oh," she replied looking up at me with those eyes that I could now tell were a clear hazel. Just as unique as she was. There was also not one drop of mascara on her lashes. This was natural. Completely natural.

"Who are you?" I asked in awe at the vision of perfection pressed against me.

She blinked several times as if she couldn't understand my words. I was almost prepared to pick her up and drag her outside to my truck with or without a name. "Harlow," she replied.

Slowly realization ran down over me like a bucket of ice-cold water. FUCK ME! *This was Nan's sister.*

RUSH

I was watching as Blaire danced with her dad when I saw Grant stalk into the ballroom like a man running from a demon. What the hell was wrong with him? I glanced back over at Blaire and she was smiling happily up at her dad talking so I left our table to go check on Grant. He was normally an even keel kind of guy. This behavior wasn't normal.

I found him as he picked up the straight shot of whiskey that the bartender sat down in front of him. He slung it back then handed the glass to the bartender and demanded another. Something had definitely crawled up his ass. "Why didn't you fucking tell me?" Grant growled without looking at me.

"What are you talking about?" I asked, watching him down another drink and ask for more.

He turned his glare towards me. "Harlow. I met fucking Harlow. You could have mentioned that Nan's sister is a

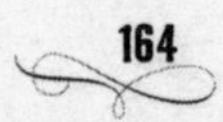

walking goddess. Mentally prepared me not to mind fuck her every way imaginable and convince my dick it was going to get some of that action before it finds out that it's impossible." He took another swig and slammed the glass down on the bar. "That's better," he sighed.

"So you met Harlow?" I asked still not following him. Why was he so pissed? I'd told him about Harlow.

"Yeah, I fucking met Harlow. Jesus, Rush, you need to warn a man first."

I was still completely confused. He had yet to make sense. "I'm gonna be honest. I don't know what the hell you're upset about."

Grant let out a hard laugh. "Fuck, you really are tied up tight by the balls," he muttered. "Since you can't seem to open your Blaire colored glasses and see other females anymore, let me clue you in. Harlow is fucking perfection. Damn Rush, her mouth," he shivered and shook his head. "God, what she could do with that mouth. And her eyes. I swear I've never seen anything like them."

So he was going on and on about how Harlow looked? "Okay. And this has you pissed off, why?" I asked thinking maybe I needed a drink for this conversation.

"Because I can't touch her and, fuck me, I want to touch her so bad. In so many, many ways. I've never been that turned on that damn fast in my life. And then to find out I can't ever touch that. Fucking sucks," he growled again.

Ah. So Harlow was the toy Grant couldn't play with. Great. I was glad she was going home in two days. I didn't need this drama. Harlow was not Grant material. She was too innocent for the likes of my brother. "Yeah, well that's a good thing because Harlow isn't your speed. You'd break her."

Grant scowled at me. "What's that supposed to mean?"

"It means that she's quiet and shy. She doesn't date. She doesn't do anything but go to school. Nothing from Kiro's world has touched her. She's polite and never wants to ruffle feathers. Even with Nan screaming at her and calling her names that aren't true, she quietly takes it and walks away. She just isn't your type. You might have a thing for her mouth but dude, she wouldn't know how to use it the way you want her to. Nor would she ever want to. She just isn't like that."

Blaire finished her dance with her dad and her eyes instantly went to my empty seat. She was looking for me. I had to go. I slapped Grant on the back. "Go find some pussy here tonight that isn't more virginal than a nun," I replied and headed back to Blaire.

She found me and smiled while I made my way to her. The music changed and Bruno Mars' song "*I Will Wait For You*" started playing over the speakers. I pulled her to me and grinned. I loved this song. I understood every word of it because it was exactly how I felt. I'd never sung for Blaire before and I was tempted to sing along in her ear but I wanted to wait. Not yet. I'd sing to her . . . but not yet.

"Did you enjoy dancing with your dad?" I asked her just so I could hear her voice.

"Yes. We talked about Momma. She'd have loved to be here. She'd have loved you. She always told me that Cain wasn't the one for me. He was too weak. That one day someone would fight for me and he'd want me more than anything else. You would have made her very happy."

My chest felt tight. I'd never been told by a female that their mother would love me. To know that Blaire felt like her mother would approve of me meant more than she knew. I remembered her mom. Not clearly but I did remember her. I remembered her smile and her laugh. She used to make me feel happy as a little boy. The smell of her pancakes made me feel safe. Knowing my son was gonna have a mother like that brought tears to my eyes. He'd have what I didn't. Something I'd only had a taste of.

"What did I say?" Blaire asked pausing as she noticed the unshed tears in my eyes I couldn't seem to control. Dammit.

"I was just thinking that my son was going to have the mother that I never got a chance to have. Your mom was special enough that her memory stuck with me." I admitted.

Blaire's eyes filled up with tears and she grabbed my face and kissed me. Her soft lips opened and her tongue slid into my mouth hungrily. Right here in front of everyone. This wasn't like her but I would take it. I started to kiss her back just as passionately when she pulled back enough so that she could look at me. Her hands still held my face. "I love you Rush Finlay. You are going to be the best husband and father the world has ever known. One day our son's wife will be thankful that her husband will have had you for a role model. She'll be lucky because of you. Because you will have raised our son to be the man that you are. He'll love her completely because he'll know how." She choked on a sob and pressed her lips to mine again and I cradled her in my arms as I enjoyed having her so determined to reassure me that I was a good man. Nothing in life was as precious as this woman. It never would be. I'd found my happiness.

BLAIRE

Bethy kissed me on the cheek then pulled something out from behind her back. A small silver package with Rush's familiar scrawl on the note that said Blaire was being held out to me. "Rush wanted to provide you with your something old," she explained.

I hadn't tried to get any of those things. I had forgotten about that tradition. Smiling, I took the package and opened it. Inside was an elegant, very expensive looking pearl ring. The silver band it was on was elegant and engraved. I held it up to see the engraving "My love" in it. That too, was old. Not something Rush had done.

A small note lay tucked beside it. I picked it up and opened it.

Blaire,

This was my grandmother's. My father's mother. She came to visit me when I was younger, before she passed away. I have fond memories of her visits and when she passed on she left this ring to me. In her will I was told to give it to the woman who completes me. She said it was given to her by my grandfather who passed away when my dad was just a baby but that she'd never loved another the way she'd loved him. He was her heart. You are mine.

This is your something old.

I love you,

Rush

I sniffed and Bethy did too. I glanced over at her and she was beside me reading the note. "Damn, who knew Rush Finlay could be so romantic," she said and sniffed again.

I knew. He'd shown me that more than once. I slipped the ring on my right hand and it fit perfectly. I figured this was not a coincidence. Smiling, I looked over at Bethy. "Thank you for everything," I told her.

She hugged me and nodded. "I should be thanking you. You're the best friend I've ever had." Before I could say more she ducked out of the room with a final wave.

I turned to look in the mirror to study myself. The pearl colored satin gathered over my breasts stayed up without straps thanks to my pregnant cup size. The waistline was high and right under my breasts and was covered in a million tiny pearls. Then the satin was covered by a layer of chiffon and hung loosely in an A frame until it hit a few inches above my knees. I'd chosen to go barefoot since I had to walk on the sand. My toenails had been painted a pale pink to match the rose petals I would walk on down the aisle.

A knock on the door startled me and I turned to see Harlow step into the room. She was holding a small box. "You look like a princess," she said smiling.

"Thank you," I replied. I felt like one.

"I have something from Rush. He wanted to be the one to supply your something new," she said and handed me the small gift. "I'd leave but I think you'll need my help."

I took the box and opened it quickly excited to see what it was he had sent up to me this time. Nestled inside was a delicate gold chain with several diamonds cut in the exact shape of my ring but much smaller. I held the anklet up and the sun coming through the windows caught the diamonds and danced around the room.

"I'll put it on you," Harlow said and I laid the anklet in her hand, then she bent down and put it around my ankle and fastened it.

I'd told Rush that I felt like I needed something on my feet but that I couldn't imagine walking in shoes across the sand. This was his answer to that. I smiled and thanked Harlow.

"You're welcome. It's beautiful on you," she said before leaving the room just as quietly as she had entered.

I looked down at my ankle in the mirror to admire it when another knock on the door came. A familiar face that I hadn't been expecting at all smiled at me and I rushed over to hug

Granny Q. I hadn't invited Granny Q because I was worried that Rush would be upset about Cain being here. I knew he'd be the one to drive his grandmother and I couldn't not invite Cain too. Tears stung my eyes as she squeezed me.

"I can't believe you're here. I can't believe you drove that far," I gushed.

She patted my back and chuckled. "Well, I didn't drive. That man of yours sent me and Cain plane tickets. First class. I've never been so pampered in my life. Was an experience I tell ya."

If I didn't already love Rush Finlay with every fiber of my being then I'd love him more for this. But he had all of me.

"Now don't you go to blubbering on me and mess up that makeup. You look like your momma. Just like her. Don't think your daddy could be happier than he is right now. I'm not supposed to come up here and make you cry. I'm here to give you something from Rush. He wanted to be the one to give you your something borrowed."

The silly smile on my face couldn't be helped. He was sending me another gift. She handed me a small box wrapped just like the one that Harlow had brought me. I took it and unwrapped it quickly.

Nestled in a satin box was a small note. I picked it up and underneath it was an old swatch of pink satin. It had been well worn and it was obviously cut from something else. I opened the note.

Blaire,

I've waited until today to show this to you. Can't say it has been easy to not say anything about it. But when I was reminded of who your mother was I was also reminded of this piece of satin. I had forgotten where it came from for a long time but I knew it was special so I kept it with me. All the time. Growing up when I was scared or alone I would hold it in my hands and rub it across my face. It was a secret I wanted no one to know about. But it soothed me. When your father reminded me of the Mickey Mouse pancakes my memories of your mother all came back. With them I remembered the day I got this piece of satin.

Your mother always wore a pair of satin pink pajamas to bed at night. She would often rock me to sleep because I was difficult to get to calm down long enough to close my eyes. I loved it when she held me. My own mother never did. I would go to sleep at night rubbing my nose across her arm and the pink satin pajamas. The day she left I remember being scared. I didn't want to be left with Georgianna. Your mother had hugged me tightly then tucked this piece of satin cut from her pajamas in my hand and told me to use it at night when I was going to bed.

I'd love to say this memory came back to me all on my own but it didn't. I just knew the fabric had to do with the woman who made me pancakes. So, I asked your dad. He told me the story and I realized that the reoccurring dream I had growing up about the woman in the pink satin pajamas was real. Not a dream. It's mine and you can't have it (unless you really want it and then it's yours).

This is your something borrowed.

I love you,

Rush

"I hope you're not wearing a lot of makeup 'cause if you are you just cried half of it off," Granny Q grumbled.

I smiled and took the tissue she was holding and wiped my face free of the tears. I wasn't wearing much makeup much to Bethy's dismay. The mascara I had on was waterproof which was a good thing. I touched the satin to my cheek once they were dry and thought of my sweet momma leaving this for Rush. Then I folded it and tucked it into my strapless bra. I took the note and went and put it away in the dresser. I wanted to keep that too. Forever.

"Well, I need to get on downstairs and get in my seat. I'll see you soon," Granny Q said and blew me a kiss before she headed out the door.

I walked over to the mirror to check my makeup when another swift knock came on the door. My dad stepped inside with a smile on his face. "You are the most beautiful woman I've ever seen. That's one lucky man down there. He just better remember it."

"Thank you, Daddy," I replied.

He slipped his hand into his pocket and pulled out another small gift box similar to the ones the others had brought in here. "I have something for you from Rush. He wanted to be the one to give you your something blue."

I couldn't keep the silly grin off my face. I had already figured out that was why he was here. Dad handed it to me. "I'll stay. You're going to need my help with it."

I opened the box excited about getting something else from Rush. A delicate gold chain that matched the anklet he'd sent me was nestled in the satin. I pulled it out and hanging from it was a topaz in a teardrop. Beside it was another note. I took it out quickly and unfolded it.

Blaire,

This teardrop represents many things. The tears I know you've shed over holding your mother's piece of satin. The tears you've shed over each loss you've experienced. But it also represents the tears we've both shed as we've felt the little life inside you begin to move. The tears I've shed over the fact I've been given someone like you to love. I never imagined anyone like you, Blaire. But every time I think about forever with you, I'm humbled that you chose me.

This is your something blue.

I love you,

Rush

I wiped another tear away and laughed. He was right. We'd had both sad and happy tears. I wanted this memory of both on me as we said "I do" today.

My dad took it from my hands and fastened it around my neck. I moved it so that it lay against my chest. I was complete.

He'd made sure I had something old, something new, something borrowed and something blue.

"It's time for us to go down now," Dad said to me before walking over to open the door. I followed him and then he led me down the stairs and out the front door. I was to walk under the house and come through an archway of pink roses and white twinkling lights. Slipping my hand into the crook of my dad's arm I let him lead me.

RUSH

I had waited at the bottom of the steps as each person came down after taking her the gifts I sent up. When her father had gone up I'd known I couldn't wait around this time. I had to get outside. I wanted to be the one taking the gifts up to her but she'd been adamant that I couldn't see her before the wedding.

Standing under the pergola covered in ivy and white roses that was placed on the sand between my house and the gulf I waited with the minister on one side of me and Grant on the other side.

"You nervous?' Grant asked.

"That she's gonna decide not to walk down that aisle? Yes," I replied.

Grant laughed and shook his head. "That's not what I meant."

"One day, brother. One day you'll understand. And when you do, I'm going to laugh my ass off."

"Not a chance in hell," he replied.

Bethy appeared under the pink roses which meant that Blaire was waiting behind her. I picked up the hidden wireless microphone that I'd had the sound guy strategically place for me and put it on my lapel. Then I reached behind the flowers and picked up my guitar. It had been years since anyone had seen me touch this thing. I could only imagine what was going through their heads. Only my dad knew what was going on because he'd helped me with the chords.

"What're you doing?" Grant whispered. The disbelief in his voice as he figured out the answer all on his own was obvious. I didn't need to tell him. As soon as Bethy was in her place I stepped in front of the minister and looked directly down the aisle. As soon as Blaire appeared the music would begin. I'd gone over everything with the sound team thoroughly.

When she stepped forward on her father's arm her eyes locked with mine and then went wide in surprise. She had been supposed to walk down the aisle to "I Won't Give Up" by Jason Mraz. But I hadn't wanted another man singing to her. Not today. I wanted her walking to me while I sang the words written just for her when she walked down the aisle to gift me with my world.

"I haven't been one much for singing . . . well, you know in front of people . . . but I figured after all we've been through. . . . this would be a good time to say what I've always wanted to say. Blaire, I love you girl . . . to the moon and back." I watched as she stood frozen looking at me. The entire place faded away and all I could see was Blaire.

When you first looked at me
and I forgot to breathe
that moment marked my hardened heart
I vowed never to leave

And the touch of your skin
healed something deep within
that left me wanting more of you
the less I got the more it grew

I couldn't help from falling for you
Oh I couldn't help from falling for you

So I'm standing here Oh Girl you know
After all we've been through we couldn't let it go
and as long as I'm alive In your eyes I'll stare
holding you so close I'll solemnly swear
that I have fallen too far, too
oh I have fallen too far, too

When I finally found you
I finally found me
that day I won't soon forget
the reason for it all

I'll give you a new name
nothing in life will be the same
the story is now complete
our life and love is all we need

Because I couldn't help from falling for you
I couldn't help from falling for you

So I'm standing here Oh Girl you know
After All we've been through we couldn't let it go
and as long as I'm alive in your eyes ill stare
holding you so close Ill solemnly swear
that I have fallen too far, too
I have fallen too far, too

My heart is beating
begging for you
this night will be
a dream come true
so fall fall fall into my arms

So I'm standing here Oh Girl you know
After All we've been through we couldn't let it go
and as long as I'm alive in your eyes I'll stare
holding you so close I'll solemnly swear
that I have fallen too far, too
I have fallen too far, too

When I played the last line, I quickly pulled the guitar strap over my head and handed it to Grant. Blaire didn't wait for any direction from the minister before she threw herself in my arms with a sob.

"That was beautiful," she said against my chest.

"Not as beautiful as you are," I replied, holding her against me.

She let out a small laugh. "I didn't know you could *do that*," she said pulling back to look up at me.

"I'm full of all kinds of exciting surprises," I assured her and winked.

"Alright you two. Let me give the girl away first," Abe said reaching for Blaire's arm and pulling her back to his side with an amused grin.

Abe kissed his daughter's cheek then looked at me. "I'd tell you how special she is but you already know that. Because you do is the only reason I can hand her over to you. I asked you to be the man I couldn't be, and you did as I asked. Not for me but for her. I couldn't be prouder of the woman she's become and the man she's chosen to spend her life with." He took Blaire's hand and placed it in mine. Then turned to take his seat.

I slipped her hand into the crook of my arm as we turned around to face the minister. She jumped beside me and looked down at her stomach with a smile. I slipped my arm around her waist and placed my hand on her stomach as our baby moved. This was mine.

HARLOW

(YES YOU READ THAT RIGHT, TOO.)

I could feel him looking at me again. I wished he would stop. Since he'd stalked off cursing a blue streak and left me standing in my hiding place at the rehearsal party, all he did was stare at me. I hated being stared at. I was ready to go home but I knew Dean was enjoying himself. I was going to see if I could get an earlier flight out. I didn't want to stay until tomorrow.

I crossed my legs again and studied my hands. No one really spoke to me and I couldn't blame them. I was boring. I never knew what to say. I was afraid to say anything. I always had been. I learned it was best to keep quiet than to say something stupid.

It was easier to blend into the background when guys who looked like Grant Carter didn't stare at you constantly. I couldn't figure out why he was staring at me. That was the craziest thing. I knew why he was upset. When you're quiet people forget you're around and they talk about stuff in front of you that really isn't your business. I'd heard Nan talking on the phone to Grant several times. I also knew that as nice of a guy as Rush was, his stepbrother wasn't. Any guy who dated someone like Nan had to be equally screwed up.

I just wish he wasn't so freaking hot. That was something I should have been prepared for. Nan was gorgeous and even though she was a raging bitch she attracted all men. Any guy that she was in a relationship with had to be equally beautiful. And oh my, was he. Very. Even his long hair that he had tucked behind his ears was attractive. Those blue eyes of his had been piercing.

It had taken two words from him and I'd become a blubbering mess. Which wasn't hard to do. I did that often. The chair beside me scraped across the floor and I jerked my gaze up to see Grant sitting down entirely too close to me. Not good. So not good. What was his deal?

"I'm sorry about last night," he snapped at me. I tensed and managed to nod my head.

Okay, so he was sorry. Fine. Now he could leave and stop looking at me.

"Come on, Harlow, say something. Give me more than a nod," he said sounding exasperated.

I wasn't sure why I should exasperate him. I hadn't done anything to him. I'd tried to stay away from him and ignore his constant staring. Even during the wedding he'd found me among the other guests and he hadn't looked away from me the entire time.

"Is it just me or do you not talk to anyone. I haven't seen you chatting it up with the other guests."

Even though I didn't like him and I sure didn't like his choice in females, I also didn't want him thinking I was an idiot. He'd go tell Nan and she'd have something else to make fun of me about. "I'm not good in crowds," I explained.

He seemed to relax some when I spoke. "This bunch is overwhelming. Can't say I blame you."

I forced a smile. It wasn't a big one but it was the best I could do. I didn't do fake well. I never had.

"You don't like me, do you?" he was obviously very observant too.

I could lie to be polite. I'd been taught by my grandmother that if I couldn't say anything nice not to say anything at all. "I don't like Nan," I replied honestly. That wasn't polite but it was true.

Instead of getting defensive Grant burst out laughing. Not a quiet amused laugh but a fully belly laugh like I was a great comedian. I watched him and hated him all the more for being attractive when he laughed. It wasn't fair. I didn't want to think anything about him was attractive.

"I'm sorry," he said, wiping his eyes and grinning at me. "But that was not what I was expecting to come out of that sweet mouth of yours. Damn, that was funny."

I didn't think it was funny at all. Did he think I was joking?

"I don't think you're alone in that, beautiful. Most people would agree with you. Especially the attendants at this wedding."

I didn't respond. He obviously liked her.

"Since you aren't going to elaborate, I'm going to assume that you aren't talking to me because I dated Nan and you don't like her."

I shrugged. Not exactly. It was more than that. Telling him was once again rude and I shouldn't be rude. But it was either be rude or let him think I was a mute. I didn't want him to make fun of me to Nan. I got enough of it from her.

"Anyone who dates Nan can't have any redeeming qualities. Or any qualities that I'd be interested in getting to know better. I don't like wasting my time with those I know I'll never speak with again." That had come out harsher than I meant for it too. Damn honesty.

Grant winced. I was acting like a bitch myself. I accused Nan of being one but I was behaving just as badly. I couldn't do that. I didn't want to be that. "Look, that didn't come out right. I'm sorry. What I meant to say is that I don't like Nan. At all. I can't see why anyone who isn't related to her would even put up with her. The fact you not only put up with her but dated her tells me that you and I would never be friends. I'm sorry. I don't want to sound like a bitch because I'm really a nice person. I just try to stay away from mean people. Nan is the epitome of mean so that leads me to believe you are mean as well. Mean people stick together." I stopped because I was making this worse. Standing up, I gave him an apologetic smile that didn't have to be forced this time because I really did feel bad for spewing from the mouth just now. I tended to do that when I tried to talk too much. Before he could say anything else I bolted. I was going to go tell Rush and Blaire goodbye and go to the airport and wait to get on an earlier flight. I would just stay the night at the airport if I had to. At least this way Grant Carter couldn't find me.

BLAIRE

"I still can't get over you singing me a song and you played the guitar. Just wow, Rush. Wow."

I was still reeling from looking up at Rush and seeing him waiting on me with a guitar in his arms. Then instead of Jason Mraz playing over the speakers Rush had sang a song that he'd written for me. After the different gifts and letters sent to my room I'd thought he couldn't top himself. I had been wrong.

"I stopped singing when I was in college. I decided that I was tired of girls being interested in me because of Dean. If I sang it only made my connection to Slacker Demon worse. So I just quit. But for you . . . I wanted you walking down the aisle to me with my voice singing words written for you. Not a generic song that is played in a million other weddings," Rush kissed the spot just below my ear. "There are no other weddings like this one and there never will be," he whispered in my ear.

I snuggled closer to him as we danced to Ed Sheeran's version of "Kiss Me" being performed by our live band. Dean had offered to get a "real band" but I hadn't wanted that. I didn't want our wedding to be more than small intimate gathering. I didn't want to make it a concert for the attending band. Rush had agreed with me and we'd found the best cover band that money could buy.

"I wish we didn't have a house full of people tonight," I said against his chest.

"Doesn't matter. We won't be there," Rush replied.

I pulled back and looked up at him. "What do you mean?"

He smirked. "You really think I'm going to share a house with all those people on my wedding night. Hell no. We have the penthouse condo at that club waiting on us when we leave here."

I was glad he'd thought of that. I didn't want to think about his dad and my dad in the same house as us tonight. "Good," I replied.

His chest vibrated from his laughter. I looked out over the other guests. All of our friends were here. Everyone we loved. Except his sister . . . and his mother. But they wouldn't have approved. Both of them hated me. Still, I felt bad that they had missed this day for Rush's sake. I just hoped one day that they would be a part of our lives for Rush. I knew even though he didn't mention them that he missed them.

"Where did you put that satin?" he asked.

I grinned and bite down on my bottom lip. "I didn't have pockets," I replied.

"I know. So where is it?"

"Tucked in my bra," I admitted.

"Guess it'll have a new meaning for me from now on," he said, teasing the bottom of my breasts with his thumbs.

"Thank you for everything. The necklace, the anklet, the ring and I'll let you keep the satin. Although I loved having it there with us. Knowing she had touched both our lives. It was perfect."

Rush tightened his arms around me. "Yeah, it was." The moment his body went tense I felt it. Gazing up at him I saw his eyes focused on something over my shoulder. I glanced back to see Cain standing there watching us. "I should probably let him dance with you. I'm trying to talk myself into it," Rush said, still holding me tightly.

I smiled at him and his torn expression. "If you don't want me to dance with Cain then I don't want to. I do need to go speak to him, and if you want to go with me and hold onto me when I do that, then you can. Relax. I'm Blaire Finlay now. The girl he loved was Blaire Wynn."

At the use of my new name his entire body relaxed and he held me tighter. "Say that again. At least the part where you say your name," he said in a husky voice.

"Blaire Finlay," I repeated.

"Damn, that sounds good," he said, pressing a kiss to my forehead. "Go talk to him. But if you don't mind . . . no dancing. I don't want his hands on you."

"So no hugging either?" I asked before walking over to Cain.

Rush frowned then shook his head. "Not if he wants to keep his arms attached to his body," he replied, causing me to laugh. My possessive man.

I walked over to Cain who stood there waiting on me with his hands stuffed in his pockets and a pained look on his face. This couldn't be easy for him. In his mind we had been forever. He hadn't really thought that Rush would be there for me in the end. He'd been wrong.

"I'm glad you came," I told him as I stopped a few feet away from him keeping enough distance to make Rush comfortable.

"Not gonna lie. I didn't want to. Granny Q made me," he replied. "But you look beautiful. So breathtaking it hurts to look at you."

"Thank you. I didn't know Rush had sent y'all the tickets and invitations until Granny Q walked into my dressing room today."

Cain nodded. "Yeah, I guessed as much. Since it was Rush inviting us and not you. Granny Q was determined we were coming once she got it."

"I'm happy, Cain."

He gave me a sad smile and nodded. "I can see that. It's hard to miss. He's pretty damn whooped himself."

There wasn't much else to say. Our time was in the past. He'd been my best friend once, but now Rush was my everything.

"Take care," I said knowing I needed to get back to Rush before he decided we'd talked too long.

"You too, Blaire. Send pictures of the baby. Granny Q will want to see them," he replied.

I turned and headed back to Rush who was standing on the edge of the dance floor with his eyes locked on me.

RUSH

Normally I spent Christmas drunk in a ski resort with whatever girl I was dating at the time and some friends. It was my go to place for the holidays. Growing up, my mother didn't decorate a tree or bake cookies. I had only seen those kinds of things on television.

The smell of pine trees, apple cinnamon, and cookies filled our house. The biggest ass Christmas tree I could find in Rosemary filled our living room and was decorated with bright colorful decorations and twinkling lights. We had a live garland and berries on our mantel and three stockings monogrammed with the letter F hung by the fireplace. Two big wreaths with red velvet bows decorated our front doors and the house was filled with Christmas carols as it played through the sounds system. Blaire had found a Christmas station on the satellite radio and she threatened me if I touched it.

Gifts with colorful paper and sparkly bows were piled up under our tree and I couldn't get rid of my friends. They were always here. Eating the sweets that Blaire kept making and drinking the apple cider that she never let get low. It was like Santa Claus had thrown up in our house. A year ago this would have sounded like hell to me. Now, I couldn't imagine ever doing Christmas any other way. This was Christmas done Blaire's way and I liked it. No, I fucking loved it. She sang along off key to the Christmas carols as she pulled cookies out of the oven and rolled those peanut butter balls in powdered sugar while I waited for her to put one in my mouth.

This was going to be what my kids grew up believing Christmas was all about and I loved it. Cuddling on the sofa watching Christmas movies and drinking hot cocoa while I laid my hand on Blaire's stomach and enjoyed feeling my boy kick. This was something money couldn't buy. Not this kind of happiness.

"Do you think we'll see your dad before Christmas?" Blaire asked walking into the living room where I stood enjoying the tree while listening to Blaire sing "*We Wish You A Merry Christmas*" off key.

"Doubt it. He just left last week," I reminded her. She frowned then nodded. "Okay. I guess we need to mail his present then. I have Harlow something too I need to mail. I was hoping you'd help me think of something for your mother and Nan. I don't know what to buy them. I've never spent time with them."

My mother and Nan? She'd bought my dad a present? And Harlow? Damn. All I'd done was buy things for her and the baby. I hadn't thought to buy anyone else something.

"Uh, yeah, um, I guess. But they won't be expecting anything. We don't really exchange gifts. It's not really a holiday we celebrate as a family."

Blaire's face fell and she looked at me with sad eyes. I didn't like seeing her sad. I liked the off key happy singing she had been doing just minutes before. "But it's Christmas. You buy the people you love things on Christmas. Doesn't have to be much. Just something. It's fun to give things."

If she wanted to give my evil mother something and my sister then I'd fucking go buy them whatever the hell she wanted me to and ship it off with a smile. "Okay, baby. I'll find them something and we can ship it off with the other things."

That seemed to appease her and she nodded. "Oh good. Okay," she started to turn around and stopped. "I have Kiro something too. We need to mail that when we mail the other things going to LA."

I couldn't help but laugh. She'd bought Kiro something. Everyone was going to think I'd lost my mind when they all got packages from me. "Kiro too. Got it," I replied.

The one good thing about Blaire's endless shopping was that it gave me time to prepare her surprise. She kept saying that after Christmas we needed to think about a nursery. I kept agreeing with her. But I also kept the last room on the left, the one with the view she loved, locked.

BLAIRE

Last year I'd let my mother sleep late because she'd been up late sick the night before. I had gotten up and fixed her favorite breakfast, strawberry waffles with whip cream, and turned on the tree lights. It would be my last Christmas with her and I had known that. I made sure everything was perfect.

When she had walked into the living room she had been greeted with a fire in the fireplace, a stocking full of her favorite splurge items, Christmas music playing, and me. She had laughed then cried and hugged me as we sat and ate our breakfast before opening gifts. I had wanted to buy her so much but money had been tight. Using my sparse creative abilities I had made her a scrap book of Valerie and I growing up. Mom had been buried with it in her hands.

This year I had done everything I could to make my mother proud of me. There were times when her favorite

Christmas carol would play and I had to fight the urge to go curl up in the fetal position and weep. But she'd made me promise her something last year. She had known it was her last Christmas too and she'd asked me to do her a favor. That next Christmas I would celebrate enough for both of us. I had tried my hardest.

My eyes had opened before the sunrise this morning and I'd eased out of bed without waking Rush. I needed some time alone. Time to process things. To remember. I knew that if Mom could see me now she would be so happy for me. I was married to the man I loved. I was going to be a mother myself and I had forgiven my dad. I held my coffee close to me and pulled my legs up under me as I sat on the sofa facing the colorfully decorated tree. This picture of my life would have been what Mom wanted for me.

I didn't wipe away the tears on my face because they weren't all sad. Some were happy. Some were thankful and some were memories.

I enjoyed the silence and watched the sunrise through the window. Rush would want me in bed when he woke up. I would need to sneak back in after I finished my coffee and brushed my teeth. This year I wanted Christmas to be perfect for him. It was our first one and this was me setting a precedence for years to come.

"Waking up on Christmas without your favorite present in bed sucks bad," Rush's sleepy voice startled me and I glanced back to see him walking into the living room. He had pulled on a pair of sweat pants but that was it. His hair was messy from sleep and his eyes were still half closed.

"I'm sorry. I was going to sneak back in bed after I watched the sunrise," I told him as he sank down on the sofa beside me and pulled me over against his side.

"I would have gotten up and watched it with you if you'd asked," he said with his chin resting on the top of my head.

I was almost positive that he would do anything I asked of him. That hadn't been why I'd left him sleeping. "I know," I replied.

Rush trailed his hand up and down my left arm. "You needed some alone time?" he asked. The understanding in his question told me that he didn't need details. He knew.

"Yeah," I replied.

"You need some more?"

"No," I said, smiling up at him.

"Good 'cause I wasn't going to go away easily,"

I laughed and laid my head back against his chest. "It's a beautiful morning."

"Yeah it is," he agreed and bent his head down to my ear. "Can I give you one of your presents now?" he asked.

"Does it require us being naked?" I asked teasingly.

"Uh, no . . . but if you wanna get naked baby, I'm always on board for that," he replied.

Surprised, I turned around in his arms and looked up at him. "You mean you want to open presents now?" I asked, thinking we would make love first.

"Not open exactly. I need to show you," he said standing up and pulling me with him.

This was not what I expected. I nodded and let him lead me back through the house and to the stairs. Maybe we were going upstairs to have sex after all?

Rush stopped at the room I'd once chosen as my own. I hadn't been in there since I had shown it to Harlow before the wedding. The door was closed and Rush stood back and motioned for me to open it. I was really confused now.

I stepped forward and turned the knob and let the door slowly open. The first thing I saw was a massive cherry wood baby bed sitting in the middle of the room with an elaborate mobile hanging down from the tall ceiling with exotic sea animals dangling from it.

Rush reached inside and flipped a switch and instead of the overhead light coming on the mobile lit up and began to play. But it wasn't a lullaby. It was the song Rush had sung to me on our wedding day. The entire mobile was lit up all the way to the ceiling. All I could do was cover my mouth in complete awe and shock as I stepped further into the room. Lights danced across the walls as the mobile spun slowly playing our song.

A rocking chair sat in the corner with a beautiful handmade blanket thrown over it. A changing table, an armoire, and even a small day bed also decorated the room. The soft blue paint on the walls was perfect considering one wall was mostly windows that overlooked the now blue sky and ocean.

I finally found my voice but all the came out was a small sob before I threw myself in Rush's arms and cried. This was perfect and he'd done this. He had chosen the perfect room for our son.

"I really hope those are happy tears because I'm gonna be honest, I was worried you'd be pissed. Bethy mentioned you might want to do this yourself and I hadn't thought about that," he said in a tight whisper.

Bethy didn't know anything. Maybe Bethy would want to do this herself but knowing Rush had taken all the time and thought for the nursery made my heart swell until I thought it was going to burst.

"This is perfect. It's beautiful. It's . . . oh Rush, he's going to love it. I love it," I assured him then I grabbed his head and pulled it down to me so I could kiss him. A fabulous magazine worthy nursery makes a pregnant woman horny. Who knew?

THREE MONTHS LATER . . .

I was a southern girl. That much was obvious. While I loved our time in New York I was glad to be back home where I could find sweet iced tea when I wanted it. Rush had missed Rosemary too. I could tell. We had unpacked and then taken all the clothes and toys we'd bought for the baby, who we still had not named, and put them in the nursery. It had been fun to hang up his clothes in the closet and fold his blankets and line up all his little shoes. We had gone a little overboard with the purchasing of clothing.

Grant had stopped by to take Rush away for some guy time on the golf course shortly after our arrival so I decided to go do some visiting. There was nothing to eat here and I was starving. Going to see if Jimmy was at the club working and getting something to eat would kill two birds with one stone. I grabbed my keys and headed outside to my car . . . or SUV . . . or whatever it was. I hadn't driven it yet. Rush had it sitting in the driveway waiting on me when we got home.

All I knew was that it was Mercedes Benz idea of a utility vehicle. I was just glad he hadn't gotten me a minivan. Apparently this one was one of the safest cars on the road. He gave me a very long sales pitch on it then told me if I didn't like it I could take it back and get what I wanted.

It was a Mercedes for crying out loud. I wasn't going to snub my nose at that. Of course I was happy with it. I just needed to figure out how to drive it. I looked down at the key he'd left me. There were directions he'd given me. I was supposed to just stick this thing that was most definitely NOT a key in my purse and carry it with me. When I touched the door handle it would automatically unlock as long as the key was on my body. Then I had to put my foot on the break and press the "on" button by the steering wheel to crank the car. Everything else should be easy enough. Yeah right.

I did as I was told and climbed into the car which isn't easy when your stomach is enormous. After buckling up I managed to crank the car without the key, which was all kinds of weird. I didn't even try to touch the stuff on the dash. It looked like something in an airplane. I understood none of it. I opened my purse and took my gun out then slipped it under my seat. I hadn't been carrying it with me since I was always with Rush. But now that I had my own car again and I would be out by myself and soon with my baby, I wanted to know there was some protection hidden somewhere. Once the baby was bigger I was going to have to find some other place to keep it. I didn't want it anywhere he could touch it. Something I needed to talk to Rush about.

Getting to the club was easy enough. The car turned off with one push of the button and I locked the doors with the thing Rush referred to as a key and headed inside.

Just as I was headed to the dinning room Jimmy walked out of the kitchen and his eyes locked with mine. A slow smile spread across his face. "Look at you, hot momma. You can even make a pregnant stomach the size of a beach ball look sexy. Go inside that kitchen and wait on me. I'll be right back," Jimmy said with a nod of his head. He was only carrying two glasses of water so he just had a quick delivery.

I opened the kitchen door and stepped inside. Several of the cooks called out greetings and I waved to them and tried to remember as many names as I could.

"Please tell me you're back in Rosemary for good now. No more running around the world. I've missed you," Jimmy whined pulling me into a hug.

"No plans to go anywhere anytime soon," I assured him.

"God, Blaire, your stomach is huge. When is this baby coming out?" Jimmy asked and started rubbing my stomach. "You can't stay in there forever, little guy. It's time you come on out. Your momma isn't that big, she can't take much more."

The kitchen door had swung open and I lifted my eyes to see a new face. She had dark brown hair and excellent bone structure. She was watching Jimmy talk to my stomach with a curious smile.

"Hello," I said, and her eyes flicked from my stomach to meet my eyes. She had gorgeous eyes as well. Where had Woods found this one and had he hired her because of her looks? Because knowing Woods he had noticed.

"Hello," she replied with a thick southern drawl that surprised me. The girl wasn't from Rosemary.

Jimmy stood back up and beamed at the girl. He liked her. That was a good sign. "Glad you're back, girl. Yesterday went to shit without you," he told her then glanced back at me. "Della, this is Blaire. She's my BFF that ran off and left me for another man. One I can't blame her for because he is one hot piece of ass. Blaire, this is Della. She may or may not be boinking the boss."

I couldn't keep the grin off my face. Yep, Woods had noticed her.

"Jimmy!" I said when her face turned beet red and realized she'd been scolding him too. I liked this girl. I just may have new friend material here.

"Woods, right? That boss," I asked, grinning because I knew there was no way she was messing around with Woods' dad.

"Of course, Woods. The girl has taste. She ain't gonna boink the old man," Jimmy replied with a roll of his eyes.

"Would you stop saying 'boink'?" Della said, still blushing. I needed to ease her embarrassment because Jimmy was only making it worse.

"Jimmy shouldn't have told me that but since he did, can I say, Woods is a great guy. If you are in fact . . . um . . . boinking him then you picked a good one."

"Thanks," she said biting back a smile. I really hoped Woods had a thing for her. I had a feeling Bethy would love her too.

"If I don't have this baby this week maybe we can get together and have lunch." I suggested. I would call Bethy and have her come too. She glanced down at my stomach and I could see that she thought it was highly unlikely that I was going to make it out the door without having this baby much less until next week. She was probably right.

"Okay. That sounds good," she replied.

I couldn't wait to tell Rush. Maybe we should invite her and Woods over for dinner one night. That would be fun.

"Della Sloane," an angry growl broke into my thoughts and I jerked my gaze from her to the police officer standing in the doorway.

"Yes, sir," she replied. I watched as her face went white and I glanced around for any sign of Woods. Where was he when you needed him? He had always been barging in at the wrong time when I worked here. Now would be a good time to barge in.

"You need to come with me, Miss Sloane," the officer barked as he held open the door waiting on Della to walk out of it. "Miss Sloane, if you don't come willingly I will have to go against Mr. Kerrington's wishes and arrest you right here on the club's grounds."

What did he just say? Arrest? Mr. Kerrington? Woods wouldn't do this. If he had he would have at least shown up and been a part of it. Besides, I was a good people reader and so was Jimmy. We both liked Della. Something was wrong.

"What are you arresting her for? I sure as hell don't believe Woods knows about this," Jimmy demanded as he stood in front of Della as if to protect her. I loved him even more for that. She looked like she was about to faint.

"Mr. Kerrington does know. He is who sent me in here to escort a Della Sloane out of the building and then arrest her once I had her in the parking lot. However, if she doesn't come willingly, I will arrest her and anyone who stands in my way."

Woods didn't know. I didn't believe him. Something was off.

"It's okay, Jimmy," she said and stepped around him. I watched helplessly as she walked out the door.

"You gotta find Woods," Jimmy said, looking back at me. "I don't believe that. I think there's more to this and I think all fingers point at the old man."

I nodded. I agreed. "I don't have Woods' number in my phone. It bugged Rush so much, I took it out," I admitted looking up at Jimmy sheepishly.

Jimmy shook his head and grinned then took my phone from my hands and punched in Woods' number. "Call him. If he doesn't answer go hunt him down. I can't help. I now have no help this shift and I gotta get my ass in gear."

I nodded and headed out the door to watch as they put Della in the cop car with way too much force than was necessary.

Woods' phone went straight to voicemail. I tried it again but again just voicemail. Running down the hall or more like waddling quickly down the hall I went to his office and knocked but nothing. I tried opening it but it was locked tightly. Crap.

I hurried outside to borrow a golf cart from Darla so I could go hunt Rush and Grant down. Woods could be with them. Just as my foot hit the stone walkway I felt a cramp followed by a gush of water between my legs. I froze.

My water had just broke.

RUSH

"You look good for a married guy," Grant teased as I walked back to the cart to get my putter.

"Of course I do. I'm married to Blaire. I'm the luckiest bastard on the planet," I replied not taking his bait. He wanted to get me fired up because Grant thought me getting angry was funny.

"Blaire is smoking hot. Even nine months pregnant," he drawled, leaning back and propping his legs up on the dash of the cart.

"If you are wanting a fucking broken nose then keep it up, bro," I snarled glaring back at him.

He began laughing and I knew he'd gotten what he wanted. I rolled my eyes. My phone started vibrating and ringing in my pocket. That was Blaire's ring. I dropped my club and reached into my pocket to get the phone. She didn't call me randomly.

If she was calling then she needed me. I started walking to the cart waiting on her to answer.

"Hey," I said the moment she answered.

"My water just broke," she said, trying to sound calm.

"I'm on my way. Stay right there. Don't move. Don't drive. Just wait on me." I took a deep breath and threw the cart in reverse and started speeding towards the clubhouse.

"I'm in the clubhouse parking lot. I was coming to find you when it happened," Blaire replied.

"I'm almost there, baby, hang on. Less than a minute, I swear," I assured her.

She made a grunting noise then took a few deep breaths. "Okay," she replied then hung up.

"Shit," I growled and wished to God this stupid cart went faster.

"I'm gathering that she's in labor," Grant replied from the seat beside me.

"Yeah," I snapped. Not wanting to talk. I just needed to get to her faster.

"I guess that means you don't care then that you just left your putter back there," Grant replied.

"Fuck, no I don't care about the damn putter."

Grant crossed his arms over his chest. "Okay, just checking."

"I need you to take my phone, get Abe's number out of it and call him."

Grant grabbed my phone and did as I asked while I slammed the cart into park and took off running across the grass to the parking lot.

Blaire was standing beside the Mercedes I'd bought her with one hand on the car and one hand on her stomach. She looked more relaxed than I imagined.

"That was quick," she smiled at me when her eyes met mine.

"Are you okay?" I asked, wrapping my arm around her and walking her over to the passenger side.

"I'm okay now. The cramping has eased up. But Rush, I shouldn't get in this car. It's brand new and I have . . . well . . . I'm wet," she said, stumbling over her words.

"I don't give a rats ass about this car. Get in. I'm taking you to the hospital."

She let me help her in the car although I could see the reluctance on her face. She didn't want to mess up her new car. I pressed a kiss to her forehead. "I swear I'll have it completely detailed inside before you get out of the hospital," I assured her before closing the door.

I ran around the front of the car and Grant was standing there with a nervous expression. "She okay?"

"She's in labor," I stated the obvious and jerked the driver's door open.

"I called Abe. What else can I do?"

"Call Dean. He'll want to know," I told him before closing the car door. I didn't let myself think about the fact I wouldn't be calling my mom or sister. There was no point. I couldn't trust them around Blaire.

"Do you think maybe you should call your mom? Or do you think she would rather not know?" Blaire asked.

I glanced over at her as I pulled out onto the road and sped to Destin where the nearest hospital was located. "I don't want them being a part of this. They don't deserve it," I replied then reached over and squeezed her hand. "This is our family now. Mine and yours. We decide who we let in it."

Blaire nodded and laid her head back on the headrest. I could tell she was having some pain from the scrunched look on her face even though she was keeping quiet about it.

"How can I help?" I asked, anxious to do something to make this stop.

"Drive," she replied with a tight smile.

She squeezed my hand tightly and let out a deep sigh of relief. "That one's over. They aren't very long or close together so we are good on time," she sounded breathless.

She squeezed down on my hand again. "Rush!"

I almost swerved off the road. "What baby? Are you okay?" my heart was slamming against my chest.

"I forgot about Della. You have to call Woods. He needs to know that the cops came and got Della."

Who the fuck was Della? Was she hallucinating? "Baby, I don't know a Della," I replied carefully in case this hallucinating thing could make her crazy. I hadn't read about this in any of those books she'd kept by the bed.

"Della is who Woods is dating. Jimmy thinks they're boinking. She was really sweet and I liked her. She looked so scared. Woods needs to help her."

She had been at the club to visit Jimmy. That's why she was

there. Not because she had been in labor. This was making sense now. "Grant has my phone. Where's yours?" If this didn't mean so much to her I wouldn't be worried about Woods' love life and his so called girlfriend being hauled in by the cops. Because that shit didn't sound promising and I didn't want Blaire around someone dangerous. But she didn't need anymore stress so I'd do whatever I could to make her feel better.

"He isn't answering his phone. It goes straight to voicemail. Who else can we call?" she asked.

I reached for her phone and dialed Grant.

"I called Dean and he's grabbing the next flight out," was Grant's greeting.

"Thanks. Listen, Woods isn't answering his phone. Call his dad. Tell him that Della," I paused and looked at Blaire who nodded that I'd gotten the name right. "Della was arrested and she needs help."

"FUCK! When was Della arrested? What the hell happened?" Grant roared in my ear. Guess he knew who Della was.

"I don't know. My wife is in labor. Just call his dad. He can find him. I gotta go."

"I'll tell him," Grant replied and I hung up.

"Woods' Dad will know how to reach him," I assured Blaire. She was frowning.

"I don't know about that but maybe I misunderstood," she stopped talking and squeezed my hand again. Another contraction.

BLAIRE

I was scared of needles. I'd decided months ago that I wouldn't be getting a long needle stuck down my back. At the moment, I was thinking that might have been a bad decision. Because I felt like my insides were being sliced open.

It didn't help that every time I needed to scream Rush completely freaked out. He needed to calm the fuck down. I had to scream to deal with this. Never again would I moan over menstrual cramps. Those were a walk in the park compared to this.

Another wave hit me and I grabbed handfuls of the sheets and let out another cry of pain. The last time the nurse checked I was seven centimeters dilated. I needed to get to ten dammit.

"Do I need to go get the nurse? Can I get you some ice? Do you want to squeeze my hand?" Rush kept asking me questions. I knew he meant well but at the moment I didn't care.

I reached up and grabbed his tee shirt and jerked his face down to mine.

"Be glad I don't have my gun because right now I'm considering the different ways I can get you to shut up. Let me scream and back off," I snapped at him and grabbed my stomach as another contraction hit.

"Time to check you again," the bubbly nurse with bright red hair pulled back in pig tails said as she all but bounced into the room. She needed to be glad I didn't have my gun too. Because she'd be next on my list.

I closed my eyes hoping I didn't have a contraction while she was down there because I may kick her in the face.

"Oh! We're sitting on ten and ready to roll. Let me get the doctor in here. Don't push," she told me yet again. I'd been told not to push for the past hour. All my body wanted to do was push. The doctor needed to hurry his ass up.

Rush was being abnormally silent. I glanced up at him and his face reminded me of a little boy's at the moment. He looked scared and nervous. I felt bad for yelling at him but the feeling didn't last when another contraction hit me, and this time it was worse. I didn't realize it could get worse.

The balding doctor walked in and beamed at me like this was a good thing. "Time to get that little guy out of there and into the world," he sounded as jolly as my nurse. Bastard.

"You can either come down here and watch, as long as you aren't queasy, or you can stay up there with her while she pushes," the doctor told Rush.

Rush stepped up to my head and reached down and took my hand in his. "I'll stay with her," he said and squeezed my hand gently.

The encouragement made me want to cry. He'd been trying so hard to make things easier on me and I had threatened to shoot him. I was an awful wife. I sniffed and he was instantly beside me. "Don't cry. It's okay. You can do this," he said looking determined and ready to go into battle.

"I was mean. I'm sorry," I choked out.

He grinned and kissed my head. "You're in a helluva lot of pain and if it makes you feel better to hit me I'd let you at me."

I wanted to kiss him but then another contraction hit me.

"Push!" the doctor ordered and I did as I was told.

Several curse words, and pushes later I heard the most beautiful sound in the world. A cry. My baby's cry.

RUSH

He was perfect. I counted all ten toes and fingers myself while Blaire kissed each one. He was also so damn tiny. I hadn't realized babies were so little.

"We have to decide on a name now," Blaire said, looking up at me after she finally managed to get our son to latch on and nurse.

We had thrown around several ideas over the past three months but nothing had seemed right. Blaire had said it was hard to name someone you'd never seen so we agreed to wait until he was born to name him.

"I know. We've seen him now. We need to give him a name. What are you thinking?" I asked her, hoping to God she didn't suggest Abraham Dean again. I loved my dad but I wasn't naming my kid after him.

" I think he looks like a Colton," she said smiling down at him. I wasn't a fan of that name.

"You still against River?" I asked.

She smiled up at me. "I want to put Rush in his name but if we name him River we can't. River Rush or Rush River sounds silly."

I'd forgot she was trying to use my name too. I wasn't going to argue with her. I liked the idea of my son having my name. "What about Cash? Cash Rush!" I teased and she bit down on her lip to keep from giggling and scaring him.

"What about Nathan, we could call him Nate?" she asked. He stopped sucking and let go to look up at her as if she'd called his name. I guess we'd come to a decision.

"Nathan Rush Finlay has a good ring to it," I agreed.

She beamed up at me happily and bent her head down to kiss his nose. "Hello Nate. Welcome to the world."

I wanted to hold him but he looked like he had decided to go to sleep instead of socialize. Blaire lifted him up and laid him on her shoulder and patted his back softly. I stood there and watched in amazement. This was mine. My family. And they were perfect.

When Blaire was satisfied with her attempt at burping him she wrapped him up tightly in his blanket and looked over at me. "It's your turn, Daddy. I need to rest. My eyes feel heavy."

I reached for him and took my son from his mother's arms. Holding him up close against my chest I inhaled his sweet baby smell. “Come on little guy. Let’s go get comfortable over there and see if we can’t find some basketball on television to watch.”

Nate slept contentedly in my arms and Blaire had gone to sleep pretty quickly after she handed him over to me. I could stay in this room with these two like this forever. Just having them close to me and knowing they were safe made everything okay.

A soft knock at the door broke into my thoughts. I turned to see the door ease open and several blue balloons enter before I saw Bethy’s head behind them. She’d stayed out as long as she could.

“Okay, Dad, I realize you’re enjoying yourself but you have to share. Both grandfathers are in the waiting room waiting patiently,” she whispered after glancing over to see Blaire sleeping.

“I don’t want to disturb Blaire. She’s exhausted. I’ll bring the baby to nursery window. Have everyone meet me there.”

Bethy looked over at the baby longingly. I knew she wanted to hold him but I wasn’t ready yet. I wasn’t so sure she wouldn’t drop him. I wasn’t so sure I could trust anyone to hold him. Snuggling him closer against me I wondered how the hell I was supposed to just let people come to my house and hold my kid.

“The nurse said y’all named him Nathan Rush. I like it,” she said.

“We’re gonna call him Nate.”

She nodded and then turned and headed back out to tell everyone where to go. I didn't mind showing them Nate through the safety of a window but I wasn't going to let them all breathe on him and touch him. Too many germs. He was too little for that shit. He needed some more meat on him before he had to deal with germs.

I stepped into the nursery and checked in with a nurse. I explained that I was there to show the baby to family members through the glass. When she turned and saw Dean standing at the window her mouth dropped open.

"Ohmygod. The Finlay baby is related to Dean Finlay? Slack Demon's Dean Finlay?"

I nodded. "Yeah. It's his grandson and I really need to show Nate here to his grandfather."

She hurried to make a path for me and followed me to the window so she could gape at my dad. Dean however was completely focused on Nate. He held up his thumb and winked at me. Abe had tears in his eyes and nodded his head. Grant was right there beside my dad grinning at Nate. Bethy was talking although I couldn't hear her but she was gushing over my boy and Jace was nodding his head in agreement.

Jimmy pushed his way through the crowd to get a look at him and put his hand on his hips and a beamed at Nate then looked at me and gave me the nod of approval. This was our extended family. We might not have siblings or mother's here with us but we had people who loved us and who would love Nate.

"Do you think I could get Dean's autograph?" the nurse asked from beside me.

"Go on out there and ask him. You're catching him in a really good mood," I told her before turning and taking Nate back to his momma.

BLAIRE

I needed to get out of the house. Rush didn't want me taking Nate anywhere, and since I was Nate's walking refrigerator, then we couldn't be separated for long. He still refused to take a bottle. I had tried pumping and feeding him but it wasn't working. He just wanted me. Which was sweet but his daddy was so dang overprotective he got pissy if people came over and wanted to hold him.

I was worried that by the time my six weeks were up and it was okay for us to have sex again Rush was going to be impossible to live with. I needed to do something to take the edge off or he was going to explode.

The first week staying home was easy. I was tired and Nate didn't sleep a lot at night so I wasn't physically able to go out during the day. I had felt bad not going to Mr. Kerrington's funeral. Woods was my friend and I hated that he'd lost his father so unexpectedly. Rush assured me when I burst into tears once I heard the news that Woods would be fine. I didn't know Mr. Kerrington so my only excuse for crying was that I was having hormonal issues called the baby blues. Or at least that is what my doctor told me.

The uncontrollable need to cry went away the day I was able to fasten my pre-baby jeans with no problem. I had gone into Nate's room and rocked him for an hour while he slept which was something his pediatrician had told me not to do. It would spoil him. It was just so hard at times. I wanted to remember these days. He would be running around the house soon enough.

When Nate turned a month old I put my foot down and told Rush it was time we went somewhere with him. Rush agreed that he had to get over it and we spent over an hour getting all his supplies together just to go eat dinner at the club. By the time we got home I was so tired I figured that maybe it wasn't worth it. We could just stay home until he was weaned. Then at that thought I promptly burst into tears because I was an awful mother.

Rush took Nate and put him to bed for me while I went to get a shower. I was behind on sleep. I needed to stop nursing Nate at night like his pediatrician suggested but I'd been weak and kept giving in. I had to stop it.

I stepped out of the shower and stood in front of the mirror. My hips were wider now. I was positive they would always be like this. I was wearing all my pre-pregnancy clothes but I didn't look like I used to look. My body was a mom body now.

"Damn. I've been trying not to look at you naked because I'm trying real hard not to resort to taking matters into my own hands but fuck . . . you're gorgeous."

Hearing the desire in Rush's voice did wonders for my self-esteem. I wanted to feel sexy again. I wanted sex again. We had two more weeks until my doctor's appointment. I wasn't sure I could last that long.

I turned around and walked over to him. Sex may be off limits but me making sure my man was happy wasn't. I leaned up on my tiptoes and pressed my lips to his and then bit down on his bottom lip. I was tired of being sweet and romantic. I wanted to be bad.

I pulled his shirt off and kissed down his chest smiling to myself as his breath hitched and he grabbed a hold of my hair. I unsnapped his jeans and pushed them down around his ankles along with his boxers. His erection stood out proudly and my mouth watered. He was so gorgeous. Even this part of him was a turn on. Slipping one hand around the base of his cock I slid the tip into my mouth and pressed it in until the head hit the back of my throat.

"*Holy fucking shit*, Blaire," Rush groaned, falling against the doorframe for support. He buried both his hands in my hair and held me there. I pulled back letting his cock spring free of my mouth with a pop and then teased the head with my tongue. His curses and moans only made me hotter.

"Suck it, please God, baby, suck it deep again," he begged, pushing my head down over him until the head once again slid into my throat. I gagged and enjoyed the groan of pleasure coming from Rush. He was enjoying hearing me gag. I was turning myself on.

I dropped my hand to slip between my legs and let Rush control how much of his cock went into my mouth with his grip on my hair. "Fucking hell, are you touching yourself?" he asked panting as he pulled back out of my mouth.

I stuck my tongue out and let his head slide off of it before nodding. Then I opened my mouth wide and stared up at him while he directed it back into my mouth. "I want to play with that pussy," Rush growled. "Don't come."

I was very close to coming so I wasn't sure I could promise him that. He began moving in and out of my mouth faster. His breathing quickened and his cursing got worse. I was about to explode.

"I need to come," he said pulling out of my mouth and I grabbed the backs of his thighs and held him there inside my mouth. "Blaire, baby, I'm gonna fucking come in your mouth if you don't let me go."

I sucked down hard on him and pumped him in and out of my mouth. I felt him tighten in against my tongue and both of his hands grabbed the back of my head. I heard the roar building inside him just before the first warm burst hit the back of my throat.

"Holy *shit*, baby. Suck it, take it . . . yeah, take it . . . *motherfucker*, that's incredible," he chanted as his body jerked under my hands and mouth.

My thighs were soaked from my excitement. I started to slip a hand down there again when Rush pulled me off his cock and picked me up and carried me to the bed and threw me down on it. I knew we weren't supposed to have sex yet but right now I didn't really care. I felt healed down there. Nothing felt different.

Rush pushed my legs apart and then his head lowered and his tongue darted out to lick the wetness on the inside of my legs. I trembled, as he got closer to my heat. "I'm gonna eat this sweet pussy until you're begging me to stop," he threatened just before he slid his tongue between my folds and then flicked his piercing over my clit. I loved the way he did that. It had been awhile. I grabbed at his hair and held him over my clit. He chuckled and the vibration made me cry out in pleasure.

"My greedy little girl," he murmured pressing kisses near my entrance before sliding his tongue inside of me and rubbing my clit with the pad of his thumb. My first orgasm hit me hard and I pulled at his hair, which made him growl hungrily and continue to lap at me.

"I want more," he whispered, grinning up at me wickedly. My legs felt like noodles as I let them fall open. "That's it. Open up," he praised me. God, I would do anything this man wanted.

In my pleased relaxed state his thumb slid inside of me and out then he let it run back until he found another hole. One I wasn't sure I wanted touched.

"Don't tense up. I won't hurt you. Just let me make it feel good," he promised. I relaxed, trusting him as he slid the tip of his thumb inside me while teasing my clit with his tongue. I caught myself pushing back on his thumb trying to get it deeper and Rush groaned in approval as he kept working his thumb in and out of my ass while he made love to me with his tongue.

There was a new kind of orgasm building. I didn't understand it but it was stronger. I wanted it. "Rush, I need," I begged not sure what I needed.

He slipped his thumb back into my wet warmth then slid it backwards again to tuck it into the tight hole that was driving me crazy. "I know what you need, sweet Blaire and I'm gonna give it to you," he said before licking me from my clit back to the small hole was he was so intent to play with. His tongue circled the hole before going back to my clit and pulling it into his mouth while slipping his thumb inside me.

I shot off. Fireworks exploded inside of me and I screamed Rush's name over and over while my body spasmed from the pure pleasure coursing through me. I'd never felt anything like it. There were no words to describe it.

When I finally came back down to earth and managed to open my eyes Rush was crawling back over my body to lie beside me and pull me against him. "I need to fuck you, Blaire. I need in so damn bad," he whispered.

I wanted him inside me. I just wasn't sure if I wanted him inside me . . . back there. His thumb was much smaller than his cock.

"I want in your pussy, Baby. Stop worrying over the other. That was just for you. I knew it would feel good," he assured me then covered us both up with the quilt and I fell to sleep quickly against his warm body.

RUSH

I reached over and turned off the monitor the minute I heard Nate start to stir. Tonight Blaire was going to get to sleep if I had to stay up all damn night walking the house with the little guy to keep his mind off eating.

I eased out of the bed and slipped on a pair of boxers and a tee shirt before hurrying downstairs before the crying started. Even with the monitor off Blaire would be able to hear him cry. I was hoping I'd exhausted her to the point that she slept through his noise tonight.

I turned on the crib mobile when I walked into the room and his fussing stopped. He liked hearing me sing. Blaire said he always stopped sucking when he heard me talk and got real still to listen. I liked that.

Walking over to the crib his little eyes locked on me and even though he wasn't exactly smiling yet you could see it in his eyes when he was excited about something. Normally Blaire's tits got him excited but then they got me excited too so I couldn't blame him for that.

"Hey buddy, when are you going to figure out that when it's dark out you're supposed to sleep?" I asked him, leaning over the crib to pick him up.

He wiggled in my arms and then moved his head so he could see my face. "You're stuck with me tonight. Mommy needs sleep even if you don't. You're wearing her out."

I left the mobile lights on and went over to the rocker and sat down with him. "We're gonna look at the moonlight over the water and rock until you decide it's time to sleep again."

Nate laid his head back on my chest when I turned him in my lap and I rocked us. I wondered what his little mind thought about the view. Did he want to go out there and touch the sand or feel the water? I couldn't wait until he could talk to me and tell me what he was thinking.

We rocked for almost an hour and I kept waiting on him to fuss for Blaire but he never did. I looked down to see his little eyelids closed and his breathing was slow and even. We'd gotten through this wakeup without mommy. I felt like I'd accomplished something.

I walked softly and slowly over to the crib and laid him back down. When I was sure he was going to stay asleep I headed back up to bed. Daddy had succeeded.

* * *

The next time Nate decided he wanted attention it was after seven in the morning. Blaire sat straight up in bed when she heard his cries and looked at the clock. "Ohmygod! Is he just now crying?" she asked, scrambling out of bed naked. I crossed my arms under my head and watched the view as she ran around the room naked looking for something to put on. I was really enjoying her new hips. They curved so damn sexy it was hard to think straight when she walked by me and they swayed.

"Actually, no. He and I had bonding time last night. I explained to him you needed some rest and he was good with it. I think he understood."

Blaire stopped searching for clothes and looked at me with her mouth hanging open slightly. "You got up with him and got him back to sleep without me feeding him? He was okay with that?"

I shrugged. "He agreed you were grumpy and needed to sleep some more."

A small smile tugged on her lips and she put her hands on those hips I was so fond of. "Y'all think I'm grumpy, huh? Last night I didn't seem very grumpy, did I? When I had your cock halfway down my throat?"

Holy hell. "Damn woman. You have to go feed our son. Don't talk like that. I'm gonna end up losing my mind before I'm given the green light from that doctor."

Blaire giggled and bent over to pick up a nightgown she'd been going to wear last night but had never gotten around to putting it on. Her ass stuck up in the air and I had to squeeze myself before I pounced on her.

The silky material slid down over her body and stopping mid thigh. She flashed me a knowing smile and turned to head towards the stairs. "I'll just take my grumpy self downstairs now," she replied.

I watched her hips sway and the nightgown clung to them with each step she took. When she had finally gotten out of eyesight I jumped out of bed and headed for the shower. I needed the coldest motherfucking shower I could stand.

BLAIRE

I put Nate down for a nap and decided to take the free time to use my yoga video I'd bought on iTunes. I needed to tighten some things up on my post baby body. Bethy told me to try yoga. Finding time to do yoga was another thing. The last time Nate took a nap and I'd tried to do yoga Rush had walked in and we'd ended up naked and on the sofa again. We had become pros at oral sex. Not that Rush needed to get any better, but it was safe to say I had learned to give a killer blowjob.

The doorbell rang before the video started so I pressed pause and went to see who it was. Rush wasn't here so it couldn't be Grant. They were together. Opening the door I thought as my eyes took in Nan that maybe I should start looking out the peep hole first. My heart rate picked up and I cursed myself because I'd left my phone lying on the floor in the game room. There were no pockets in my yoga pants.

"Is Rush here?" she snapped. I mentally cringed. He wasn't here and I wasn't sure I should let her inside. But then did I not let her in? She was Rush's sister.

"He left with Grant a couple of hours ago. Something to do with Woods," I was talking too much. That wasn't her business.

"Are you gonna let me in? Or should I come back later?" the disgusted tone of her voice at the idea I had the power to not let her inside what was now my house was obvious. I didn't want to let her in but then Rush would want to see her. He'd just mentioned her a few nights ago. He was wondering how she was and telling me his mother said she was out of the clinic and doing better.

Going against my better judgment I stepped back to let her inside. "Come on in," I said, hating the idea of being alone with her. My gun was in the car although I really didn't think I'd need that. She wasn't that kind of dangerous . . . I didn't think.

"So how's it feel being Mrs. Finlay?" she asked. Her tone indicated that she wasn't happy about it and that this was not a friendly question.

"Wonderful. I love your brother," I replied.

"You can't lie to me. I'm not fooled by the innocent look. You got knocked up so you could snag him. He wasn't gonna ignore his kid. You figured that out and used it. I just hope the kid's his." The hate laced in her words made me wince.

I really wanted to call Rush and get him home. I didn't want to talk to her. Not if this was going to be a Blaire bashing conversation.

"I'm sorry you feel that way. When you see Nate you'll see there is no doubt who he belongs too. He is Rush's mini me." I was mad at myself for taking her bait and defending myself. But I did.

At the mention of Nate I could see Nan wince. She either hated the idea that we had a child or she hated that it was also my kid and she didn't want to feel connected to it. I wasn't sure. "I'm going to go grab my phone and call Rush to let him know you're here. Please help yourself to something to drink or eat if you want it. You know where everything is."

I started for the stairs.

"Wait. I don't want to see Grant. Tell him not to bring Grant," she said in a tight voice.

"Okay. I will," I replied. I was pretty sure Grant didn't want to see her either but I wasn't about to let her know I knew all about that. I wasn't touching that issue.

I hurried up the stairs and went to get my phone. I would call Rush then go check on Nate . . . maybe I could kill all the time alone with her up here hiding. Picking up the phone I dialed Rush's number.

"Hey baby, everything okay?" he asked when he answered.

"Um . . . depends on what you consider okay," I said. "Your sister is here."

"Turn around man. I need to go home now," Rush said to Grant. "I'm on my way. Is she okay? Is she being nice? Did you let her in?"

"Yes, no, not really and yes," I replied.

"She's not being nice. Shit, Blaire. I'm sorry. Why'd you let her in?"

"Well, because Rush, she's your sister. I wasn't going to refuse to let your family in your house."

Rush took a deep breath. I knew what that meant. He was frustrated. "Blaire. If I ever hear you call that my house again I am going to go apeshit. That is our house. Our fucking house. If you don't want to let someone in then don't. Call me and they can wait on the damn steps until I can get there. I just want you comfortable in your home."

"Okay. Well, I let her in because you love her and I love you. How's that for a reason?"

Rush let out a low chuckle. "Nan is and will probably forever be the one person I love that I don't expect you to be nice to. She needs to earn that shit. She hasn't. You blow her off, kick her ass out, whatever you want to. Don't you put up with her mouth spewing bullshit."

I decided I wouldn't tell him about her accusation that Nate might not be his. He'd lose it. "Just hurry," I begged.

"Five minutes away," he promised.

I hung up and slipped the phone into my sports bra this time before going to check on Nate. Opening the door slowly I peeked in to find him kicking and gurgling at the sea creatures hanging from the mobile. Smiling, I walked over and his little eyes shifted until they locked on me. He kicked harder at the sight of me and my heart squeezed.

"That was not a very good nap," I told him leaning over to

pick him up. "I didn't even get to do any yoga and mommy's bottom needs some yoga."

His little head tried to bury in my chest. It wasn't time for him to eat but when he woke up he wanted in my shirt. Just like his dad. Grinning, I walked him over to the changing table and put a fresh diaper on him while he fussed. He hated having his diaper changed.

I picked him up and kissed his puckered up lips. The tears stopped and he opened his mouth trying to get something to eat again. "Not now mister. You just ate an hour ago," I told him before heading out the door.

I didn't want to take him downstairs. I was afraid of what Nan would say about him. I didn't think I could deal with it if she was mean to my baby. The front door chimed and I let out a sigh of relief. Rush was home.

"Daddy's home," I whispered.

I carried Nate downstairs and listened for Rush and Nan's voices. It wasn't hard. She was already raising her voice. Rush must have come in correcting her for making me feel uncomfortable. I decided against taking Nate into the kitchen to hear his dad yelling at Nan. We went out the front door. Nate loved going outside and watching the waves. The sea breeze would drown out all Nan's angry words.

We walked under the house and out towards the beach.

"Blaire, could you bring Nate up here?" Rush asked, looking down at me from the porch. Apparently he wanted Nate around Nan. I understood him wanting his sister to meet his kid but she hated the momma so this might not be wise. I paused and looked down at Nate.

The mommy in me wanted to take him and run back upstairs and lock ourselves safely inside his room. But he was Rush's child too. I pressed a kiss to his temple. "Daddy's sister Nan isn't very nice. You're going to have to learn to overlook her," I whispered in his ear more for my sake than his since he had no idea what I was saying. When I reached the top step Rush was waiting on me. "If you want me to take him and you not go in there I will. But if you want to go in there I swear to you that she will behave or I'll throw her out of this house."

I wasn't about to send my baby to see the big bad wolf and not go with him. If he had to face Nan, so did I. I held him tighter to me and shook my head. "I want to be with him."

Rush nodded. I could see by the look on his face that he understood. He opened the door for us and stepped back so I could walk inside with Nate.

Nan was sitting on a bar stool with a pissed snarl on her face. She spun around and her eyes went to Nate. I could see the moment she saw that each small feature was Rush's. He didn't even have my eyes. He was all Rush.

"Guess he is yours after all," she said. I stopped and took a step back bumping into Rush's chest. His arm came around me and he held me there.

"You wanted to see him. Be careful what you say to his mother. Apologize for that last stupid ass remark or I'm going to walk you to the door."

Nan's eyes flared with fury and I had a feeling Rush had just started something we really didn't need in our home. But she took a deep breath and lifted her eyes full of hate to me. "I'm sorry," she snapped. She didn't mean it but the fact Rush had made her say it was worth it.

"Can I hold him?" Nan asked, lifting her gaze to Rush's.

I went stiff as a board. If he told her yes I was making a run for it with Nate. There was only so much he could ask of me.

"Probably not a good idea. With you glaring at his momma like that I don't think she's gonna feel safe handing him over."

Nan scowled. "He's your kid too."

"He is. But Blaire is his mother. I don't let anything happen that she isn't comfortable with."

"God, Rush, where did your balls go?"

"That's strike two, sis."

Nan rolled her eyes and stood up from the stool. She looked back at Nate and her eyes softened a little. He was hard not to love. He was as beautiful as his father. "Mom would love to meet him," Nan said, pulling her purse strap up on her arm. "You should at least send her a photo."

"Mom didn't give a shit about her own babies, Nan. You know that. Why would she care about mine?"

Nan didn't flinch. She only shrugged. "Good point."

Nate started to fuss in my arms. He was trying to get to the goods again. I shifted him in my arms and Rush reached for him. "Give him to me. He won't be thinking about milk when I've got him."

I handed Nate to him and he instantly calmed down and stared up at Rush. He was fascinated with his father.

"You're good with him. I'm not surprised. You've been playing dad for as long as I can remember," Nan said. It was the first nice thing she'd said since she'd gotten here.

"I'm only good at it because I've watched Blaire. She's taught me everything."

Nan didn't like that answer and it wasn't true. He'd been a natural from day one. I started to argue when Nan pushed her stool back scrapping it across the floor. "I just wanted to see the kid and let you know I'm doing better. If you want to see me, I'm in town for a few days. I'm not up for anymore bonding with your little family here so keep that in mind."

I watched as she stalked out of the kitchen and down the hall towards the front door without another word. Rush didn't respond.

"And she's still a bitch," Rush muttered.

I turned to look up at him and he was frowning. "I'm sorry that she talked to you like that," he said.

"I ignore everything she says. She wants me to be the villian and I'm afraid she always will. It's okay. I didn't marry her," I replied.

Nate heard my voice and he moved his head to look at me before he started crying. He wanted me for my boobs. I smiled and reached out to take him. "I'm going to have to just feed him again. He must not have gotten full last time. He's determined to eat again."

Rush handed him to me. "Lucky little shit."

I kicked him and he laughed that full belly laugh that I loved.

"You hungry?" he asked.

"Yes. Starving. Can you make me a sandwich?" I asked him before walking to the living room to go get comfortable in the recliner.

"Anything for you," he replied.

RUSH

Woods was standing outside of the clubhouse arguing with that Angie or Angel or Angelina . . . hell, I couldn't remember her name. She'd been around off and on through the years. I was pretty sure she was a summer fuck for Woods when we were in high school. Her daddy was in the same business as the Kerringtons and Grant had thought that Woods was going to marry her.

Then this Della chick had shown up and my guess was things had changed. Or not. I couldn't tell. Last I'd heard Della hadn't gone to jail and it had been a misunderstanding. Woods had raised some hell though at the police station. The girl had her hands on Woods' arms and it looked like she was begging him. I wasn't sure I wanted to walk up in that conversation but the dude looked like he needed help.

He had enough shit to deal with now that his dad was dead.

No one had been prepared for it and Woods had it all thrust at him overnight.

"Get off me, Angelina. I swear to God if you don't leave me the fuck alone I'm going to have a restraining order on your ass," Woods said as he shoved her hands off him. He turned to see me walking up and the relief in his eyes was obvious. "Rush. Hey, you here for that meeting?" he asked.

I had no idea what he was talking about and I was willing to bet he'd just made that shit up. "Yep," I replied.

"This isn't over, Woods. I swear to you it isn't. You're making a huge mistake," she cried out as Woods broke free from her and started towards me.

"Get me the hell away from her. Fast," he muttered as he walked past me. I turned and followed him. I'd been here to talk to Bethy about babysitting tomorrow night so I could take Blaire out on a date. But it looked like I was going to get to chat with Woods first.

He opened the door to the club and went inside not waiting to see if I followed him. "Craziest fucking bitch I've ever met," he swore once we were both safely inside. He ran his hand through his hair and let out a frustrated growl. "I was running. I was. I was gonna pull a fucking Tripp. I was taking Della and we were going to leave this shit behind. My dad had pushed me too far and I was done. Then he had to up and die. Come to find out the will stated that on my twenty-fifth birthday this place became mine. My grandfather had made it very fucking clear and it was so locked up my dad couldn't budge it. I can't run now can I? It's all mine. The grandfather I loved and admired hadn't screwed me over after all. But God it's all so screwed up now. I just need to focus on getting Della better. I don't have time to handle all this. I know nothing, Rush. Motherfucking NOTHING. My dad didn't let me into the business side of it. He said I had to earn my place," Woods let out another frustrated sigh and started pacing the floor.

I wasn't sure what all he was talking about but the dude had problems. Grant was the guy he needed, not me. I wasn't someone to share your shit with. I didn't do heart to hearts.

"Woods?" A petite brunette with big blue eyes walked inside the door looking right at Woods with a concerned frown. "What's wrong?"

The man morphed right in front of me. He took two long strides and pulled her into his arms like someone was about to touch her and he needed to make sure she stayed safe. "I'm fine. Did you get to sleep late?" he asked in a tender voice that I swear to God I'd never heard the dude use.

She nodded and slipped her arms around him. "Yes. Everything was fine this morning. Stop worrying," she told him. She turned her head and looked over at me.

"Della, this is Rush Finlay. You met his wife, Blaire. Rush, this is my Della."

His Della. Oh man, that was what was wrong. He'd been sunk. I couldn't keep the grin off my face. I understood that feeling completely. And damned if it didn't make me happy that

Woods was wrapped up in another woman and wasn't sniffing after mine anymore. Thank you, Della.

"It's nice to meet you," she said.

"Nice to meet you too," I replied. She had no idea just how nice. Good Ole Woods Kerrington was in love. Funniest shit I'd heard all week.

BLAIRE

Bethy was waiting on me at the club for drinks. I had fed Nate and left him with Rush so that I could go have some girl time. She also wanted me to officially meet Della. I waved at Jimmy as I passed by the kitchen and hurried into the dinning room.

Della and Bethy were over by the windows that overlooked the gulf. Della turned and smiled at me when she noticed me approaching. I wasn't sure exactly what happened with the police, I just knew that it had been a very bad misunderstanding and rumor was that Woods threatened the officer that did it at the police station. Grant said he'd thrown him up against the wall. Reminded me of something Rush would do.

"About time you got here. I was about to have my second mimosa without you," Bethy said cheerily.

"Sorry, I had to feed Nate before I left him. He was more

hungry than normal. But you know I can't drink mimosas. I'm nursing. However, I will take a tall glass of orange juice."

"Nursing does not sound fun at all. Except for those amazing knockers you have, I see no reason to do it," Bethy replied.

I chose to ignore her. She wouldn't understand. Instead, I looked over at Della. "I'm glad we are finally getting to talk," I told her.

"Me too. I'm sorry about the last time we met. I can't imagine what you thought of me after," she stopped and trailed off.

"I thought that there had been a horrible mistake and while in labor I ordered Rush to get in touch with Woods and let him know there was an emergency," I assured her.

Della let out a sigh. "Yeah, it was a crazy day. But thank you. I didn't know until later that you'd gone into labor that day."

Bethy ordered another mimosa for herself and Della. I told the new waitress that I just wanted orange juice.

"So, you aren't working for Woods anymore I hear," Bethy said to Della.

She frowned and shook her head. "No. He won't let me. He likes to keep me with him most of the time. We're dealing with some things . . ." she trailed off again. I could tell she didn't want to talk about her personal life and I couldn't blame her. She'd just met us.

"I can't keep you bitches in the kitchen. What am I supposed to do if all my good help keeps hooking up with the rich ass men in this club and leaving me behind?" Jimmy said as he pulled out the fourth chair at the table and sat down.

"I still work here," Bethy reminded him.

"You don't work in the kitchen so you're no help to me. I'm almost scared for Woods to hire any more attractive females. I need someone helping me that doesn't catch these horny ass sexy fuckers' eye," Jimmy hissed then winked at us.

I looked around the table and smiled. A year ago I was lost. I didn't have anyone. Walking into Rush Finlay's house that night had changed everything. I sat back and listened as Jimmy told us about his bad date the night before and how he wanted in Marco's pants. Marco was apparently the new chef. Bethy had agreed that Marco's pants were very fine. I looked across the table at Della was smiling as she listened to them talking and I recognized that look. I think she'd found a home too.

"So, Blaire, how's the sex after marriage and baby. We gotta know, girl. Is Rush Finlay still smoking up the sheets?" Jimmy asked his eyes twinkling with anticipation. He had a serious crush on my husband.

"Not your business, Jimmy. You need to move on from your fascination with my man. It's too late now. I have him," I replied.

"Hell, you're no fun. I just want details. Really descriptive details. What about you Della? Wanna tell me how the boinking is with Woods? Is he all bossy and shit? That just sounds hot."

Della's face turned bright red and she laughed. "I'm not going there with you either, Jimmy," she replied.

Jimmy stood up and stuck out his bottom lip. "And here I always thought female gossip was naughty and fun. Y'all are boring me to tears," he waved a hand dramatically at us before turning and heading back to the kitchen.

"Now he's gone I'd like to know how sex is with Rush and Woods," Bethy said with a smirk.

I shook my head and glanced over at the door as Grant came sauntering in by himself. He looked like he was deep in thought. He hadn't been around lately and I figured it was because he was out of town again. Something looked like it was bothering him. He glanced up and his eyes met mine.

A small smile touched his lips and he winked before walking over and taking a seat at a table by himself.

"Grant's back in town for the summer. He seems different though," Bethy said apparently thinking the same thing I was.

"Yeah, he seems off," I agreed.

"You play with fire and you get burned. Nan is all kinds of screwed up. She had to fuck with his head. I still can't believe they were messing around though," Bethy whispered.

"Nan came by the other day," I said looking back at Bethy then Della. "She still hates me."

Bethy sniffed. "Who cares? Bitch."

Della's eyes went wide and I realized we were talking about people she didn't know. It was rude.

"So, Della, I've been gone and I missed all the action. So tell me, how exactly did you meet Woods? By working here?"

Della shook her head and smirked. "Not exactly. We met

back in September . . . it was . . . kind of a one night stand," she said, her cheeks turning bright pink.

This was going to be juicier than I thought. "Oh, this sounds fun," I replied and leaned forward to hear the rest of it.

Nate was now taking a bottle. Bethy's aunt and my old boss Darla had agreed to babysit for us so we could go down to the club's bonfire tonight. It was the kick off to the summer season and it was a members only event. Rush hadn't wanted to go but Bethy had called and begged. I felt guilty for not having enough time to spend with her anymore so I'd talked him into it.

Tomorrow was my doctor's appointment and Rush's patience was very thin. I was expecting him to go with me then attack me in the parking lot. I wouldn't complain but I wasn't going to give him any ideas.

Grant had called to see if we were going and so had Woods. He'd wanted to see if I would help keep Della company in case he had to deal with anything during the bonfire. Bethy was also supposed to be sticking close to her. They'd become friends, which only confirmed my belief that she'd be a good friend. Bethy was picky.

The fire was larger than any other bonfires on the beach because the city couldn't control what happened on club property the way they could the public beach. Bethy had said this party was the don't miss of the season. Which sounded good to me. Rush and I needed to get out.

"You sure you don't want to go change into something else before we get out of this car?" Rush asked looking over at me.

Frowning I looked down at my new outfit. I'd bought it last week. It was a white linen skirt that hit mid thigh and a pale yellow off the shoulder top that just met the waist of my skirt. It only flashed skin if I raised my arms. "You said that at the house. Do you not like it?" Maybe my body wasn't ready for me to wear something like this yet.

Rush grabbed my chin and locked his gaze with mine. "You're mouthwatering, Blaire. I don't like knowing that other men are looking at you."

Oh. Well in that case. "I am sure I don't want to change. I like it when you get all possessive. Turns me on," I told him with a wink and opened my door.

"You're killing me woman," he said with a slam of his door.

Rush reached down and took my hand in his as we walked down to the beach. The sun had already set but the bonfire lit up our path once we got halfway. Bethy was waving at us and jumping up and down as soon as we stepped into the light.

"Guess she wants us to come over there," Rush said with an amused tone.

"Good guess," I replied.

Bethy was already three sheets to the wind when we got over to them. Jace only rolled his eyes when she staggered over to hug me. She smelled like tequila. "Hey you, you're late!"

"No they're not. You just started drinking the hard stuff right off the bat and now you're too drunk to know how long we've been here," Jace piped up from his seat. He also looked a little annoyed with her.

I glanced around for Della but I didn't see her. "Where are Della and Woods?" I asked Bethy who smiled at me like she had no idea who I was talking about.

"I saw them a little bit ago but Woods had to deal with some of the staff smoking pot. Not sure what happened to Della," Jace said.

Crap. We were supposed to be watching out for Della. "I might need to go look for her," I whispered to Rush.

"I'll go with you. Not sure I want you walking around alone," he said.

"No. Just sit and visit with Jace. Get a drink. I'm just going to make one big sweep of the area and come back. You don't have to come with me."

Rush frowned and I pushed him towards the free chair beside Jace. "Go," I ordered and looked back at Bethy. "I'm gonna go find Della," I told her.

"Me too! I wanna go too!" Bethy said, raising her hand like she was in school.

"Nope. Your drunk ass is staying right here," Jace replied.

Bethy stuck out her bottom lip and plopped down on Jace's lap. "You're no fun," she whined.

I didn't wait on her to ask again. I turned and made my way down closer to the fire. I saw several familiar faces. I got a hug from Jimmy and met his date for the night but I still didn't see Della. I circled around and headed up to the outer reaches of the bonfire light to see if she was hiding in the darkness. I didn't see anyone.

I started to turn around and head back to Rush when I heard a high pitch voice screeching. It wasn't a frightened voice more like one that was upset about something. I took a step closer to the parking lot and heard another voice, definitely female and very southern, trying to calm the other voice down. I glanced back in the direction I'd left Rush and he didn't see me.

I headed back to the parking lot following the voices. The closer I got I could make out more words. There wasn't anyone in the parking lot so where were they? I walked over to where we had parked our car and stopped.

"No, please. Just, talk to Woods. I didn't do anything. I swear. Don't, oh god," the softer voice was scared.

"I'm done talking to Woods. You took what was mine. He chose you. Fine. He can have your skanky crazy ass. But first you're gonna fucking pay for taking what was mine." A loud slap and a cry of pain followed her words. "Hurts don't it, bitch. You're a psycho. Why Woods thinks you can make him happy I don't know. He'll learn. He will fucking learn to screw with me," the angry female said again and another cry of pain came from who I now knew was Della. I had no idea who the other woman was though but she was hurting Della. I thought about going to get Rush but then she could have seriously hurt her by then.

I didn't need Rush. I wasn't sure who the psycho was but I could handle her. I reached into my purse and pulled out my key and quietly unlocked the door. Slipping my hand under the seat I pulled out my gun and checked the safety.

I didn't intend to shoot anyone. Just needed to scare the bully off and then call Woods. Hopefully she hadn't hurt Della too bad. Another cry from Della made me move faster. I followed the voices around a building.

I saw the other woman first. She was holding Della by the hair and calling her crazy again. She was real hung up on the fact she thought Della was crazy. This bitch was pissing me off.

I held the gun and pointed it at the woman before letting her know she had company.

"Let her go," I said and watched as the woman spun around still holding Della's hair in her grasp. Della let out another sob.

"What the fuck?" the woman said, looking at me like I was the one who was crazy.

"Let go of her hair and step away from her," I said loud and clear so she didn't misunderstand.

She laughed. "That's not even real. I'm not an idiot. Go mind your own fucking business and stop playing Charlie's Angels."

I flicked safety off and cocked the gun. "Listen, bitch. If I wanted to I could pierce both your ears from here and not mess your fucking hair up. Go ahead, test me," I kept my voice even and cold. I wanted her to believe me because I really didn't want to have to shoot at her to prove my point.

Her eyes went wide and she dropped Della's hair. I watched Della move away from her quickly from the corner of my eye.

"Do you have any idea who I am? I could end you. Your ass is going to sit in jail for a very long time for this," she snarled, although I could hear the fear in her voice.

"We're in the dark and there are three of us. You don't have a scratch on you. Della's bleeding and bruised and it is our word against yours. I don't care who you are. This doesn't look good for you."

She moved back away from me some more keeping her eyes on my gun. "My daddy will hear about this. He'll believe me," she said with a shaky voice.

"Good. My husband will hear about it too and he'll sure as hell believe me."

The woman let out a hard angry laugh and shook her head. "My daddy can buy this town. You have fucked with the wrong woman."

"Really? Bring it on 'cause right now you're looking at a woman with a loaded gun that can hit a moving target. So please . . . Bring. It. On."

Della was curled up with her arms wrapped around her knees as she sat silently watching us.

"Who are you?" the woman asked for the first time taking me seriously.

"Blaire Finlay," I replied.

"Shit. Rush Finlay has married a hick with a gun. I find this hard to believe," she spat.

"I'd believe her. She's holding the fucking gun, Angelina," Rush's voice came from behind me.

The woman's eyes went wide. "Are you kidding me? This town is insane. All of you."

"You were the one beating up an innocent woman over a man in the dark," I reminded her. "You're the one who looks insane here."

The woman held up her hands. "Fine. I'm over this. I'm done," she yelled and walked up to the parking lot. I lowered the gun and put the safety back on before handing it to Rush then running over to Della. Her big blue eyes were wide with disbelief.

"Did you really just hold a gun on her?" she asked with awe in her voice.

"She was putting a beating on you," I reminded her. She buried her face in her hands and let out a shaky laugh. "Ohmygod. She's crazy. I swear I was beginning to think she was going to beat me until I was unconscious. I kept thinking I was going to zone out and then she'd really hurt me," she glanced up at me. "Thank you."

I held my hand out to her. "Can you stand up? Or do you want to sit here while I call Woods?" She slipped her hand in mine.

"I want to stand. I need to stand up," she said.

I pulled her up. "You got a phone?"

She nodded and pulled one out of her pocket. I waited while she dialed Woods.

"Hey."

"Actually, no not really. I had an incident with Angelina."

"No . . . no . . . she's gone. Uh, Blaire showed up and . . . uh scared her off."

"Blaire is still here and so is her husband."

"Behind the parking attendant building."

"Okay. I love you too."

She hung up and looked up at me through thick eyelashes. "He's on his way."

"Good. We'll wait with you." I opened my purse and pulled out a wet wipe. I was a mommy now so I had those on me at all times. "You want to clean the blood off your lip before he gets here and goes after Angelina?"

Della nodded and took the wipe from me. "Thanks."

I turned around to look at Rush who was watching me closely but not speaking.

Two headlights came barreling up the road and slammed on their breaks just beside where we were standing. Woods jumped out of the truck and came running down to where I stood with Della.

"Dammit!" he roared pulling her into his arms. "God, baby I am so sorry. She's gonna pay for this," he assured her as his hands ran over her checking her to make sure she was okay.

"It's okay. I think Blaire scared her," Della said against his chest. Woods looked back at me and frowned.

"What did Blaire do?" Woods asked.

"She pointed a gun at her and threatened to pierce her ears," Della said.

Woods cocked and eyebrow. "So, Alabama pulled her gun out again? Thanks, Blaire," he said before kissing Della's head and whispering into her hair words that were not meant for anyone else.

"I'm glad I found them. You need to do something about that woman, she's a crazy bitch," I said before turning to walk back to Rush. He slipped his hand around my waist and held me against him.

"Thank you," Della called out.

"You're welcome," I replied then Rush and I turned to head back to towards the parking lot.

"I'm not gonna be able to wait until tomorrow. You fucked that up when I came around the corner and you were standing there like a badass holding a gun on Angelina. I think I may have come in my damn jeans when you told her you could pierce her ears from there. I'm fucking that sweet little badass pussy tonight."

I tried to bite my lip to keep from laughing but I couldn't.

Rush grinned. "Glad you agree there's no more waiting. I'm ready to get lost up in my heaven again."

I stopped walking and stood on my tiptoes to kiss his cheek. "I love you Rush Finlay."

"Good 'cause I'm not ever letting your sexy ass get too far away from me again."

"How far is too far?" I asked

"It's all too far. I want you right here beside me . . . forever."

GRANT

The banging on my door sounded like a damn freight train. I pushed the covers off me and looked over at Paige. I'd brought her home with me last night from the bonfire. We'd both had too much to drink and we had plenty fun before we passed out. That much I could remember. Paige was always nice and easy. She didn't do the clingy thing.

The banging kept on. I grabbed my discarded shorts from last night and pulled them on before walking down the hall towards the door. "Shut the fuck up! Dammit, that's too fucking loud," I yelled before opening the door. The sun was up and right in my eyes. I threw my arm over my eyes and squinted while calling whoever was at my door a crazy motherfucker.

I didn't do hangovers well.

"Aren't you charming this morning," Nan drawled as she

pushed past me and walked in. Shit. Not who I wanted to deal with this morning.

I slammed the door. "What do you want, Nan? It's ten fucking a.m." I growled.

Nan walked into my kitchen and leaned against the bar.

"I need a place to stay," she said in a softer voice that she only used when she wanted something. A year ago that shit worked with me. I was so wrapped up in her selfish ass I couldn't see straight. It was all the sex though. She was good at it. A fucking gymnast in the bed. I learned the hard way that sex didn't make up for heartbreak and bitch. I was done with her. With all of it.

"Call Rush. I'm going back to bed. You know the way out," I replied heading back to my bedroom.

"I can't! He won't help me. I can't stand Blaire and he knows it. He loves her more than me. She took him away from me. She took everything away from me. I hate her and I can't pretend to like her. But I don't have anywhere to go. I don't want to live with my mother. I want to come back to Rosemary."

"Sucks for you. Bye Nan." I opened the bedroom door and walked over to the bed and laid face down.

"Paige? Really Grant? You don't know where all that has been. You've stooped pretty low. Even for you."

Paige sat up rubbing her face and I enjoyed the fact she was naked and Nan was getting a very good look at her tits. They were a helluva lot nicer than Nan's.

"I stepped up. Last chick I fucked was you," I replied. She'd walked into that one.

Paige looked at me then Nan with bloodshot eyes. I was pretty sure she'd been smoking pot last night. "What the fuck?" she grumbled pulling the sheet up to cover herself.

"Nan's here to make my life hell. Ignore her," I said rolling on my back and propping my hands behind my head.

"Really? This is what we've become?" Nan asked.

"This is what you made us, Nan. You wanted to screw around, well I agree. It's fun. Thanks for the idea."

"Paige, for godsake get some clothes on and leave. We're trying to have a conversation," Nan snapped at Paige who was sitting quietly listening to us.

I reached over and patted her leg. "Don't leave. Her ass has been shown the door. She needs to take it," I told Paige. I really had rather they both leave but I wasn't an ass. I wouldn't kick Paige out. I'd let her leave on her own.

"For real? You're gonna just whore around and not even let me explain? Did you know I was in a rehab? Did you care? You sure as hell didn't call me. No one did. Not even Rush."

I felt a small pang for her but it was really small. Sometimes I still saw that little girl who wanted someone to want her so bad. Those were the times I had compassion. Then I remembered the bitch she had become and decided she deserved what she got.

"When you dish shit out you get shit back. That's what my grandaddy always told me. Maybe somebody should have taught you that too. Saved us all a fucking load of trouble."

Nan pointed at Paige. "Leave. Now."

I grabbed Paige's arm. "Ignore her."

Paige looked back and forth between the two of us and then shook her head. "You two are all kinds of fucked up. I think I'll go home and get some rest. My head can't take this," she started to get up then reached over and kissed my cheek before crawling out of the bed naked.

I admired her ass while she got her clothes on for Nan's sake not because I really wanted to. I was too tired to think about naked females.

Paige waved bye to me then hurried out the door carrying her shoes. I had no idea where her car was but that didn't matter right now. She lived two floors up in the same condo complex as I did. Which was another reason she was handy.

Nan walked over to the bed and sat down.

"Get off my bed, Nan. I swear to God I'll tell you every detail of what Paige and I did on these sheets last night if you don't get your damn ass off my bed," I warned. I couldn't really remember exactly what we did last night. But Nan didn't have to know that.

"You're disgusting," she screamed standing up and glaring at me.

"Yeah, so are you. At least I know Paige. She's not some girl I just plucked off the damn street to fuck."

Her eyes flashed with unleashed fury. I'd called her shit. She'd wanted to push me away and she'd succeeded. I had seen enough. I wasn't interested anymore.

"You said you loved me," she reminded me.

"I thought I might love you, Nan. But then I woke up and realized a hot fuck and good pussy isn't love. It's just really good sex."

The hurt look in her eyes should have made me feel guilty but it didn't. I had confused need and want with love. I didn't know what it was like to love someone. Not the way Rush loved Blaire. I'd never felt that. I knew that now. I had no fucking clue and I was pretty damn sure I never would.

"Fine. You want to hurt me then do it. I deserve it," Nan spat, standing up and walking back to the door. "But this isn't over, Grant. I can admit that I messed up. You just need to admit that you still have feelings for me."

Did I? I wasn't sure I did. I was angry at her for jerking me around but I wasn't sure there were feelings left.

"I am working through some things. It would be nice if someone gave a shit and understood."

I would not let her turn this around on me. I hadn't asked for this shit. I'd tried to make it work. She'd refused to ever be more than a fuck buddy. I had wanted more and she'd made it clear that I could easily be replaced.

"I don't think I'm the one to help you, Nan. Problem is I know what your life was like and I know why you're a bitch. But unlike Rush, I don't let that excuse fly. It's time you stopped using it and changed. You're pushing everyone away. Do you want to end up like your mom?"

She stiffened and I knew I'd hit a nerve. Without a word she spun around and stalked out of my condo slamming the door behind her. Good fucking riddance.

Now I could get some sleep.

Chapter One

JAX

This was it. Finally. The last stop on my tour. I shoved open the door to my private suite, and Kane, my bodyguard, closed it firmly behind me. The screaming on the other side of the door had only made my head hurt. This had been fun once. Now all I could think about was getting away from it. The girls. The relentless schedule. The lack of sleep and the pressure. I wanted to be someone else. Anywhere else.

The door opened and quickly closed behind me. I sank down onto the black leather sectional sofa and watched my younger brother, Jason, as he grinned at me with two beers in his hands.

"It's over," he announced. Only Jason understood my feelings lately. He'd been with me through this crazy ride. He saw my parents' need to push me and my need to push back. He was my best friend. My only friend, really. I gave up trying to figure out who liked me for my money and fame a long time ago. It was pointless.

Jason handed me a beer and sat down on the sofa. "You killed it out there. The place was insane. No one would ever guess you were looking forward to running off to Alabama in the morning to hide away all summer."

My agent, Marco, had told my parents about the private island on the Alabama coast. They were so ready to have somewhere other than our house in LA that they'd jumped at the idea.

Going back to my hometown—Austin, Texas—hadn't been something they wanted to do. Too many people knew who we were.

The security Sea Breeze offered had always allowed me the freedom I'd lost when the world had embraced me. For a few weeks every summer we were a family again. I was just another guy, and I could walk out to the water and enjoy it without cameras and fans. No autographs. Just peace. Tomorrow we were headed back there. It was our summer break. But this year I was staying the whole damn summer. I didn't care what my mother or my agent thought I should do. I was hiding out for three months, and they could all kiss Marco's ass. What had started as my mother's insistence that we spend the summers together in Alabama had become mine. I needed time with just them. I rarely saw them the rest of the year. It was the only house we had to call ours. I had my house in LA, and my parents and Jason had theirs.

"You're coming down, right?" I asked him.

Jason nodded. "Yeah. I'll be there, but not tomorrow. I need a few days. Mom and I had an argument about college. I want to give it a few days before I face her again. She's driving me crazy."

Our mother was a micromanager when it came to our lives. "Good idea. I'll talk to her. Maybe I can get her to back off."

Jason laid his head back on the leather. "Good luck. She's on a mission to make me miserable."

Lately I felt like she was doing the same to me. I no longer lived with her. I lived independently. I was the one who paid her bills. Why she thought she could still tell me what to do was beyond me. But she did. She always thought she knew what was best. I was done with that, and so was Jason. I'd talk to her, all right. She needed to remember who was actually in control here and back off.

"Take a few days. Enjoy yourself. Let me prep Mom for the fact that I'm not going to allow her to control your life. Then come south," I told him before taking a long drink of my beer.

SADIE

"Mom, are you going to work today?" I rolled my eyes at my very pregnant mother, who lay sprawled out on her bed in her panties and bra. Pregnancy made Jessica an even bigger drama queen than before having unsafe sex with another loser.

She moaned and covered her head with a pillow. "I feel awful, Sadie. You just go on without me."

I'd seen this coming a mile away before school even let out. The last day of school landed yesterday, but instead of being able to go out and be a normal teenager, I was expected to make the money for us. It was almost as if Jessica had planned on me working in her place all along.

"I can't just go to your workplace and take your position. Haven't you explained the situation to them? They won't be okay with your seventeen-year-old daughter doing your job."

She pulled the pillow from her face and tossed me a sulk she'd perfected years ago. "Sadie, I can't continue cleaning house with my stomach the size of a beach ball. I'm so hot and tired. I need you to help me. You can do it. You always figure stuff out."

I walked over to the air conditioner and turned it off. "If you'd stop running it at a continuous sixty-eight degrees, we might be able to get by on less money. Do you have any idea how much it costs to run a window unit all day long?" I knew she didn't know, nor did she care, but I still asked.

She grimaced and sat up. "Do you have any idea how hot I am with all this extra weight?" she shot back at me.

It took all my restraint to keep from reminding her that she got this way because she hadn't used a condom. I bought them for her and made sure her purse always contained several. I even reminded her before she went out on dates.

Remembering who the adult was in our relationship could be difficult at times. Most of the time it seemed to me our roles were reversed. Being the adult, however, did not mean she made smart decisions, because Jessica simply did not know how to be responsible.

"I know you're hot, but we can't spend every dime we make on the air conditioner," I reminded her.

She sighed and flopped back down on the bed. "Whatever," she grumbled.

I walked over to her purse and opened it up. "All right, I'm going to go to your job today, by myself, and I hope they allow me inside the gate. If this doesn't work, don't say I didn't warn you. All I am qualified for is minimum-wage jobs, which won't pay our bills. If you would come with me, I would have a better chance of landing this position." I knew as I spoke the words that I'd already been tuned out. At least she had managed to keep the job for two months.

"Sadie, you and I both know you can handle it by yourself."

I sighed in defeat and left her there. She would go back to sleep as soon as I left. I wanted to be mad at her, but seeing her so big made me pity her instead. She wasn't the best mom in the world, but she did belong to me. After I got my clothes on, I walked past her room and peeked through the door. She softly snored with the window unit once again cranked to sixty-eight degrees. I thought about turning it off, but changed my mind. The apartment already felt warm, and the day would only get hotter.

I stepped outside and got on my bike. It took me thirty minutes to get to the bridge. The bridge would take me from Sea Breeze, Alabama, onto the exclusive island that was connected to it. The island wasn't where the locals lived, but where the wealthy came for the summer. Jessica had managed to snag a job as a domestic servant at one of the houses that employed full staffs. The pay was twelve dollars an hour. I prayed I would be able to take over her position without a hitch.

I found the address on her employee card I'd retrieved from her purse. My chances of getting this job were slim. The farther I pedaled onto the island, the larger and more extravagant the houses became. The address of my mother's place of employment was coming up. She, of course, had to work at the most extravagant house on the block, not to mention the very last one before the beach. I pulled up to a large ornate iron gate and handed Jessica's ID card to the guy working admittance. He frowned and gazed down at me. I handed him my driver's license.

"I'm Jessica's White's daughter. She's sick, and I'm supposed to work for her today."

He continued to frown while he picked up a phone and

called someone. That wasn't a good thing, considering no one here knew I was coming in her place. For good. Two large men appeared and walked up to me. Both sported dark sunglasses and looked like they should be wearing football uniforms and playing on NFL teams instead of black suits.

"Miss White, can we see your bag, please," one of them said, rather than asked, while the other one took it off my shoulder.

I swallowed and fought the urge to shudder. They were big and intimidating and didn't appear to trust me. I wondered if I seemed dangerous to them, all five feet six inches of me. I glanced down at my skimpy white shorts and purple tank top and wondered if they'd considered the fact that it would be impossible to hide weapons in this outfit. I thought it somewhat strange that the two big guys were reluctant to let me in. Even if I happened to be a threat, I do believe either one of them could have taken me blindfolded with his hands tied behind his back. The image popped into my mind and made me want to laugh. I bit my bottom lip and waited to see if dangerous little me would be allowed entrance through the bigger-than-life iron gates.

"You're free to enter, Miss White. Please take the servants' entrance to the left of the stone wall and report to the kitchen, where you will be instructed how to proceed."

Who were these people who needed two men the size of Goliath to guard their entrance? I got back on my bike and rode through the now open gates. Once I made it around the corner, past lush palm trees and tropical gardens, I saw the house. It reminded me of houses on *MTV Cribs.* I never would've guessed houses like this even existed in Alabama. I'd been to Nashville once and seen houses similar in size, but nothing quite this spectacular.

I composed myself and pushed my bike around the corner, trying to not stop and stare at the massive size of everything. I leaned my bike against a wall, out of sight. The entrance for the servants was designed to impress. At least twelve feet tall, the door was adorned with a beautifully engraved letter *S*. Not just tall, the door was really heavy, causing me to use all my strength to pull it open. I peeked inside the large entry hall and stepped into a small area with three different arched doorways ahead of me to choose from. Since I'd never been here before, I didn't know where the kitchen might be located. I walked up to the first door on the right and looked through the opening. It appeared to be a large gathering room, but nothing fancy and no kitchen appliances, so I moved on to door number two, peeked inside, and found a large round table with people sitting around it. A large older lady stood in front of a stove unlike any I'd ever seen in a house. It was something you'd find in a restaurant.

This had to be the place. I stepped through the arched opening.

The lady standing noticed me and frowned. "Can I help you?" she asked in a sharp, authoritative tone, though she kind of reminded me of Aunt Bee from *The Andy Griffith Show*.

I smiled, and the heat rose, threatening to spike out the top of my head as I watched all the people in the room turn to face me. I hated attention and did whatever I could to draw little to myself. Even though it seemed to be getting harder the older I got. As much as possible, I tried to avoid situations that encouraged other people to speak to me. It's not that I'm a recluse; it's just the fact that I have a lot of responsibility. I figured out early in life that friendships would never work for me. I'm too busy taking care of my mom. So I've perfected the art of being uninteresting.

"Um, uh, yes, I was told to report to the kitchen for further instructions." I quietly cleared my voice and waited.

I didn't like the once-over the lady gave me, but since I was here, I had no choice but to stay.

"I know *I* sure didn't hire you. Who told you to come here?"

I hated all those eyes on me and wished Jessica hadn't been so stubborn. I needed her here, at least for today. Why did she always do these things to me?

"I'm Sadie White, Jessica White's daughter. She . . . uh . . . wasn't well today, so I am here to work for her. I'm . . . uh . . . supposed to be working with her this summer."

I wished I didn't sound so nervous, but the people stared. The lady up front frowned much like the way Aunt Bee looked when someone made her angry. It was tempting to turn and run.

"Jessica didn't ask about you helping her this summer, and I don't hire kids. It ain't a good idea with the family comin' down for the whole summer. Maybe during the fall when they leave we can give you a try."

My nervousness from being the center of attention immediately disappeared, and I panicked at the thought of our losing this income we so desperately needed. If my mom found out I couldn't work for her, she would quit. I pulled my grown-up voice out of the closet and decided I needed to show this lady I could do the job better than anyone else.

"I can understand your concern. However, if you would give me a chance, I can and will show you I'm an asset. I'll never be late to work and will always complete the jobs assigned to me. Please, just a chance."

The lady glanced down at someone at the table as if to get an opinion. She moved her eyes back up to me, and I could see I'd broken through her resolve. "I'm Ms. Mary, and I'm in charge of the household staff and I run the kitchen. You impress me and you have the job. Okay, Sadie White, your chance starts now. I'm gonna team you up with Fran here, who has been working in this home as long as I have. She'll instruct you and report back to me. I will have you an answer at the end of the day. Here is your trial, Miss White. I suggest you don't blow it."

I nodded and smiled over at Fran, who was now standing.

"Follow me," the tall, skinny redhead who appeared to be

at least sixty-five years old said before she turned and left the room.

I did as instructed without making eye contact with any of the others. I had a job to save.

Fran walked me down a hallway and past several doors. We stopped, opened one, and stepped inside. The room contained shelves of books from the floor to the ceiling. Large dark-brown leather chairs were scattered around the room. None faced any of the others or looked to be used for any type of visiting or socializing. The room was clearly set up to be a library. A place where people could come, find a book, and lose themselves in one of the large cushy chairs.

Fran swung her arm out in front of her, gesturing to the room with a bit of flair. It surprised me coming from an older lady. "This is Mrs. Stone's favorite spot. It's been closed off all year. You will dust the books and shelves, clean the leather with the special cleaner, and clean the windows. Vacuum the drapes; clean and wax the floors. This room must shine. Mrs. Stone likes things perfect in her sanctuary. I will come get you at lunchtime, and we will dine in the kitchen."

She walked to the door, and I heard her thank someone. She stepped back inside, pulling a cart full of cleaning supplies. "This will have everything you need. Be careful with all framed artwork and sculptures. I warn you, everything in this house is very valuable and must be treated with the utmost care. Now, I expect you to work hard and not waste any time with foolishness." The tight-faced Fran left the room.

I circled around, taking in the extravagance of my surroundings. The room wasn't really big; it just seemed full. I could clean this. I hadn't been asked to do anything impossible. I went for the dusting supplies and headed to the ladder connected to the bookshelves. I might as well start at the top, since dust falls.

I managed to get everything dusted and the windows cleaned before Fran returned to get me for lunch. I needed a break and some food. Her frowning face was a welcome sight. She moved her gaze around the room and nodded before leading me in silence back down the same path I'd taken this morning. The smell of fresh-baked bread hit me as we rounded the corner and stepped into the large, bright kitchen. Ms. Mary stood over the stove, pointing to a younger lady, who wore her hair in a bun covered with a hairnet just like Ms. Mary's.

"Smells good, Henrietta. I believe you've got it. We will test this batch out on the help today, and if everyone likes it, you can take over the bread baking for the family's meals." Ms. Mary turned, wiping her hands on her apron. "Ah, here is our new employee now. How are things going?"

Ms. Fran nodded and said, "Fine."

Either this lady didn't smile much or she just didn't like me.

"Sit, sit. We have much to get done before the family arrives."

I sat down after Fran did, and Ms. Mary set trays of food in front of us. I must have been doing something right since Fran directed her words in my direction. "All the help eat at this table. We all come at different shifts for lunch. You may choose what you want to eat."

I nodded and reached for the tray of sandwiches and took one. I took some fresh fruit from a platter.

"The drinks are over there on the bar. You may go choose from what's there or fix something yourself."

I went over and poured some lemonade. I ate in silence while I listened to Ms. Mary direct Henrietta as they baked bread. Neither Fran nor I made any attempt at conversation.

After we were done, I followed Fran to the sink, where we rinsed our plates and loaded them into the large dishwasher ourselves. Just as silent, we returned to the library. I was a little less nervous now and more interested in my surroundings. I noticed the portraits as we walked down the hallway. There were portraits of two very cute little boys. The farther I walked, the older they seemed to get. Toward the arched entrance that led to the hallway where the library was located, an oddly familiar face smiled down at me from a life-size painting. A face I'd seen many times on television and in magazines. Just last night during dinner he had been on television. Jessica watched *Entertainment Daily* during our meal. Teen rocker and heartthrob Jax Stone was one of their favorite topics. Last night he'd had on his arm a girl rumored to be in his new music video. Fran stopped behind me. I turned to her, and she seemed focused on the portrait.

"This is his summer home. He will be arriving with his parents and brother tomorrow. Can you handle this?"

I simply nodded, unable to form words from the shock of seeing Jax Stone's face on the wall.

Fran moved again, and I followed her into the library. "He's the reason teenagers are not hired. This is a private escape for him. When he was younger, his parents insisted he take a break each summer and spend time with them away from the bright lights of Hollywood. Now he's older and still comes here for the summer. He leaves now and then to go to different events, but for the most part, this is his getaway. He brings his family with him since they don't see each other much during the year." Fran paused dramatically and then continued. "If you can't handle it, you will be fired immediately. His privacy is of the utmost importance. It's why this is such a high-paying job."

I straightened and grabbed the bucket I'd been using. "I can handle anything. This job is more important to me than a teenage rock star."

Fran nodded, but from her frown, I could see she didn't believe me.

I focused more energy into my work. At the end of a long day, I listened while the quiet, frowning Fran reported to Ms. Mary. She believed I would be a good worker and I should be given a chance. I thanked her and Ms. Mary. I figured I should be able to save enough money for the fall, when my mom would have the baby and not work, and I would be back in school. I could do this.

Yes, Jax Stone was famous, had incredible steel-blue eyes, and happened to be one of the most beautiful creations known to man. I made myself admit that much. However, everyone knows beauty is only skin deep. I assumed the shallowness radiating off of him would be so revolting I wouldn't care that I cleaned his house and passed him in the halls.

Besides, guys were a species I knew nothing about. I never took the time to talk to one even when they did their best to talk to me. I've always had bigger problems in life, like making sure we ate and my mom remembered to pay our bills.

When I thought of all the money I'd wasted on the condoms I'd shoved into Jessica's hands and purse before she went out with the countless men who flocked to her, I really had a hard time not getting angry with her. Even in thrift-store clothing, she looked gorgeous. One of her many disgusting men told me I'd inherited the cursed looks. From her curly blond hair to her clear blue eyes and heavy black lashes, I somehow managed to get it all. However, I had the one thing I knew would save me from certain disaster: My personality came across as rather dull. It was something my mother loved to remind me of, yet instead of being upset by it, I held on to it for dear life. What she thought of as a character defect, I liked to think of as my lifeline. I didn't want to be like her. If having a dull personality kept me from following in her footsteps, then I would embrace it.

The apartment we lived in for almost five hundred a month sat underneath a huge old house. I walked in after my first day of work to find that Jessica wasn't inside. With only four rooms, she couldn't have gotten far.

"Mom?" I got no answer.

The sun was setting, so I stepped out onto what Jessica referred to as a patio. If you ask me, it was really more like a small piece of slab. She loved coming out here to look out over the water. She stood out in the yard with her increasing stomach on view for all to see, in a bikini I'd bought at a thrift store a few weeks ago. She turned and smiled. The facade of sickness from this morning no longer appeared on her face. Instead, she seemed to be glowing.

"Sadie, how did it go? Did ol' Ms. Mary give you a hard time? If she did, I sure hope you were nice. We need this job, and you can be so rude and unsociable."

I listened to her blabber on about my lack of social skills and waited until she finished before I spoke. "I got the job for the summer if I want it."

Jessica sighed dramatically in relief. "Wonderful. I really need to rest these next few months. The baby is taking so much out of me. You just don't understand how hard it is to be pregnant."

I wanted to remind her I'd tried to keep her from getting pregnant by sacrificing food money to buy her some stupid condoms, which didn't help at all! However, I nodded and walked inside with her.

"I'm starving, Sadie. Is there anything you can fix up real fast? I'm eating for two these days."

I'd already planned what we would eat for dinner before I got home. I knew Mom was helpless in the kitchen. I'd somehow survived the early years of my life on peanut butter and jelly sandwiches. Somewhere around the time I turned eight, I realized my mother needed help, and I began growing up quicker than normal children. The more I offered to take on, the more she gave me. By the time I turned eleven, I did it all.

With the noodles boiling and the meat sauce simmering, I went to my room. I slipped out of my work clothes and into a pair of thrift-store cutoff jean shorts, which happen to be the core of my wardrobe, and a T-shirt. My wardrobe was simple.

The timer for the noodles went off, letting me know the food needed to be checked. Jessica wasn't going to get up and help out anytime soon. I hurried back into the small kitchen, took out a spaghetti noodle on a fork, and slung it at the wall behind the stove. It stuck. It was ready.

"Really, Sadie, why you toss noodles on the wall is beyond

me. Where did you get such an insane idea?"

I flipped my gaze up and over at Jessica. She was kicked back on the faded pastel couch, which had come with the apartment, in my bikini.

"I saw it on the television once when I was younger. It has stuck with me ever since. Besides, it works."

"It's disgusting, is what it is," Jessica mumbled from her spot on the couch.

She couldn't boil water if she wanted to, but I decided to bite my tongue and finish with dinner.

"It's ready, Mom," I said as I scooped a pile of spaghetti onto a plate, knowing she would ask me to bring her one.

"Bring me a plate, will ya, honey?"

I smirked. I was a step ahead of her. She rarely got up these days unless she absolutely had to. I slipped a fork and spoon onto the plate and took it to her. She didn't even sit up. Instead, she placed it on the shelf of a belly she'd developed, and ate. I placed a glass of sweet iced tea down beside her and went back to fix my own plate. I'd worked up an appetite today. I needed food.